OPERATOR 5:
PATRIOTS' DEATH MARCH

SECRET SERVICE #5™
OPERATOR 5
AMERICA'S UNDERCOVER ACE

PATRIOTS'
DEATH MARCH

By Curtis Steele

POPULAR PUBLICATIONS • 2022

CHAPTER 1
"WE WHO ARE ABOUT TO DIE!"

O N A ridge overlooking the Arkansas River, four batteries of Central Empire field artillery were masked behind a camouflaged screen of high-banked snow.

Gunners stood ready, waiting for the word to fire. Sixteen guns were trained on a single spot in the Arkansas River.

Some fifty feet behind the gun batteries stood a small group of Central Empire officers, while their Commander-in-Chief, Marshal Kremer, focused a high-powered telescope upon that point in the river at which the guns were aimed. There was a mellow glow of satisfaction on the harsh features of Marshal Kremer. He was the man who had led the well-trained, thoroughly-equipped, goose-stepping troops of the Central Empire to almost complete victory over two-thirds of the earth's surface. Europe and Asia had fallen before the combination of Kremer's brilliant strategy and the Central Empire's powerful military machine.

Now, after nine months of ceaseless campaigning, all that portion of the United States east of the Rocky Mountains was in the hands of the invading Central Empire. The American Defense Forces were offering a last-minute, bitter resistance to the conquering cohorts in the snow-packed reaches of the Rockies. But the huge guns and impregnable tanks of Kremer's invading forces were proving too much for America.

Nine months earlier, the first troops of the Central Empire had landed in Canada after conquering Europe and Asia. Those troops had marched down through the United States almost without opposition, and had swept all resistance from the Atlan-

Like a thunderbolt he hurled himself at the Purple troopers, with the solid phalanx of horsemen pressing behind him.

tic seaboard as far south as Florida. Then, inexorably westward they had worked their way, burning, ravaging, torturing and killing.

Rudolph I, Emperor of the Central Empire, master of Europe and Asia, was bent upon making himself the undisputed lord of

America. That end was almost in sight for Rudolph. Only one area of resistance remained within the occupied territory. That was the organized incursion which had recently been made into the occupied territory by a small but determined group of patriots under the leadership of a man who was known as Operator 5. Formerly an ace of the American Intelligence, Operator 5 was now desperately battling the entrenched might of the Central Empire with every weapon of wit and cunning at his command.

Only a few short weeks before, Operator 5 had led this small band of patriots across half the continent into the heart of the enemy territory in the steel district surrounding Pittsburgh. Here, the Central Empire was manufacturing the huge guns with which it proposed to blast the American Defense Force out of the Rocky Mountains and back into the Pacific Ocean. Those guns were being forged out of iron which was dug from American mines, by the sweat of American forced labor. The huge blast furnaces and coke ovens of the Pittsburgh district were manned by captive Americans, forced to work under threat of torture and death to themselves and their families.

Operator 5 had struck a telling blow by wrecking the entire industrial district around Pittsburgh. To do that he had been forced to destroy a huge dam on the Ohio River and flood the entire countryside. While the Central Empire troops were thrown into panic by the sudden bursting of the mighty Maximilian Dam, Operator 5 had gathered together as many American volunteer patriots as he could find, and had loaded upon commandeered trucks a treasure in guns, munitions and other supplies.

These guns and munitions, if they could be brought across the country to the American Defense Forces in the Rocky Mountains, would serve to stem the tide of the Purple Invasion. And though it seemed at first glance to be a hopeless task, they had so far traversed almost a third of the distance. American civilians in the occupied territory, hearing of this incredibly daring undertaking, had flocked to join Operator 5. They were pathetically glad of an opportunity to risk their lives in any undertaking against the brutal conqueror.

With the aid of these volunteers, who had spread out on either side of the line of march as a shield against the troops of the Central Empire, Operator 5 had led his long, unwieldy caravan to the banks of the Arkansas River. And now, while his men labored at the erection of pontoon bridges across the river, an unknown peril menaced the caravan from the ridge to the north. MARSHAL KREMER kept his telescope fixed upon the progress of the pontoon bridges. There were four of them going up, about a hundred feet apart; and the four batteries of field artillery had been carefully laid by the Central Empire gun captains, so that the first thundering barrage would sink those four bridges in the swirling river.

Marshal Kremer chuckled softly. He addressed an officer who stood behind him, in the uniform of a major general of the Central Empire.

"We will let them finish the bridges, General Kurtz, and let them begin to cross. Then we will open on them." He jerked a thumb toward the plain behind the ridge across the river where a vast sea of helmets stretched out as far as the eye could reach.

Those helmets were the headgear of the massed infantry of a whole division of the Central Empire Fifth Army Corps. They were being held there in reserve, out of sight of the Americans, ready to attack the moment the order was given.

Kremer went on: "As soon as they have begun to cross, General Kurtz, we will open up on them with all four batteries. The eight batteries hidden back along the road will also open up upon the main column of the American trucks. The barrage will continue for fifteen minutes, after which you will order your first brigade to attack. The second and third brigades will circle and attack the rear guard of the American column. They will then move forward to meet the First Brigade near the river. By the time they meet, the Americans should be entirely annihilated. You understand, General Kurtz?"

General Stepan von Kurtz was a small, extremely thin man with such a large moustache, trimmed in the imperial manner, that his face seemed to be suspended from the moustache instead of the moustache from his lip. He smiled fawningly at Kremer, and bowed from the waist.

"Your tactics are, as usual, most brilliant, my dear Marshal. These fools of Americans should be wiped out to the last man. How they expected to cross the entire country, literally surrounded by our own troops, is beyond my comprehension. This Operator 5 must indeed be a fool—"

Marshal Kremer stopped him with an abrupt gesture. "No, Kurtz, he is not a fool." Kremer's rough-hewn, granite-like face softened for an instant. "I admire Operator 5 above all others of the Americans. Had it not been for him, this country would have been subjugated six months ago.

"This undertaking of his to transport guns and ammunition across two thousand miles of our territory may seem mad to us; it seems to be doomed to failure before it has well begun. Yet I feel that Operator 5 must have some trick up his sleeve, as these Americans say. He knows very well that he cannot get through with those trucks. He must know that every move which his column has made since leaving Pennsylvania has been observed. He must know that somewhere along the route he will be ambushed, for he cannot think that we will let him through. Yet he goes on, like a stubborn fool."

Kremer frowned, and tapped the be-medaled chest of General Kurtz with a gnarled forefinger. "But I know he is not a stubborn fool, Kurtz. He has some trick, some plan. I can hardly believe that he lays himself open to annihilation in this way."

Kurtz shrugged. "All men make mistakes, Herr Marshal. Operator 5 is, no doubt, desperate, willing to try anything. He must know that those new guns which were manufactured for us in the Skoda plant in Czechoslovakia have already been landed, and are speeding westward on railroad trains. Once those guns are in position, the Americans are lost. He must be anxious to reach his own people in the Rockies with whatever supplies he has."

"Perhaps," Marshal Kremer said reflectively. "Nevertheless, von Kurtz, I am waiting to see what trick he will play. Go back to your men now. In a moment I will give the order to open the barrage. You will be ready to send your men in to the attack as soon as the barrage lifts."

Von Kurtz saluted, turned on his heel and left. Kremer lifted his telescope once more, and continued his inspection of the pontoon bridges which were being swiftly placed across the river, below. He chuckled.

"It's too bad, Operator 5," he murmured half to himself, "that you have to fall into this trap. In a few minutes your column will be no more!"

He raised his hand, called to the officer in charge of the battery: "Be ready to fire at the signal. In a moment it will be time!"

DOWN IN the valley, at the river crossing, the American engineers were working on the pontoon bridges as if they were entirely unaware that grim death was staring down at them out of the muzzles of the field pieces hidden on the ridge.

The huge, unwieldy caravan of trucks, loaded with guns, ammunition and supplies, stretched out for miles back on the road. The column was a humming beehive of activity. But a very strange thing might have been observed by any Central Empire spy who had the opportunity to come close enough to those trucks.

Such a spy would have noticed that not a single one of the huge guns being transported in the trucks was in condition for service. Their breechblocks were smashed and twisted. And the ammunition trucks seemed to move lightly over the bumpy road, as if the cases they contained were empty.

The faces of all the Americans in the column were grim,

determined, and they seemed to be rather careless about the way they handled the vehicles containing cases of high explosives.

Many of the trucks were out of gasoline, and the Americans were pushing them along over the snow-covered road.

A Central Empire spy, observing all this, might have wondered why these Americans were so grimly intent upon crossing the country with a column of trucks that contained nothing but useless guns and empty boxes of ammunition. This spy would have been unpleasantly enlightened had he been able to overhear the conversation which was at that moment taking place some three miles to the rear, at the tail of the column.

Here, three men and a boy stood in the road alongside a field where an airplane had just descended to a perfect three-point landing. One of the three men was the aviator who had arrived in the plane. The second man was the one who was even at that moment the subject of the conversation at the crest of the distant ridge between Marshal Kremer and General, von Kurtz. He was Jimmy Christopher, known in the records of the United States Intelligence as Operator 5. The third man was Frank Ames, a young American who had aided Jimmy Christopher in getting together this huge caravan.

The boy, who seemed to be participating in this conversation without question from his elders, was no more than fifteen or sixteen. Lively eyes, in a freckled, hump-nosed face, proclaimed the intelligence of this boy, and gave an inkling of the reason why he was included in this conference.

The lad's name was Tim Donovan; and he had accompanied Operator 5, sharing his perils, his victories and his misfortunes for the last three years. One day, long before the Purple Invasion, Operator 5 had met a ragged newsboy on the lower East Side of New York City; that newsboy had rendered Operator 5 a signal service; and ever since that day the two had been inseparable. Operator 5 had taught Tim Donovan out of the vast store of his own experience. He had taught the lad to drive a car, to pilot an airplane, shoot with rifle or revolver, as well as a dozen other accomplishments which many a mature man might have envied. And the clever Irish lad had proved an apt and willing pupil. He assimilated everything that Jimmy Christopher taught him, and he made an invaluable assistant.

Many times, his native wit and intelligence had gotten them both out of tight situations. So that now, at a critical time in American history, Tim Donovan was included in his own right, in a conference of his elders.

The pilot of the airplane was speaking swiftly, making a concise report to Operator 5.

"I've just flown clear across the State of Missouri, and over the Ozarks, Operator 5. I spent an hour flying over the right of way of the old Missouri Pacific Railroad. My plane was painted to resemble a pursuit ship of the Central Empire, and they didn't bother me. There are ten supply trains moving westward, just east of the ruins of the town of Sedalia. Each train has fifteen cars. The first five trains are carrying big guns—each gun mounted on an armored car of its own. The second five trains are loaded with ammunition. They're moving slowly, at about twenty-five to thirty miles an hour, and at that rate they shouldn't reach Kansas City for about five hours."

Jimmy Christopher nodded. "That's about where I thought they'd be, Kelton. Now, what about the Central Empire troops? Have they got many men in that section?"

Kelton, the aviator, shook his head. "There're only about two companies of infantry in Sedalia, and when I flew over Holden, I saw a whole division pulling out. It was moving south. I guess it's hurrying to intercept this column of yours. Operator 5, I've got to tell you, you're in a trap."

Kelton flung his hand in a wild gesture toward the ridge not far distant, upon which the screened batteries were hidden. "There's almost a whole army corps hidden behind those hills. I'm almost sure I spotted some camouflaged guns on that ridge back there. And as I flew over the Ozarks, I noticed that every road was filled with motorized troops. They're pushing south as fast as they can. Operator 5, this column can never get through. You'll be outnumbered fifty to one. They'll capture every gun and every bit of supplies that you've got in these trucks—"

KELTON PAUSED, looking with puzzled expression at the amused grins upon the faces of Frank Ames and Tim Donovan. "What's so funny about that?"

"We've kept this a very carefully guarded secret, Kelton, but as a matter of actual fact, this whole column is only a hoax. We spiked every gun, and we've moved all the ammunition and supplies out of the trucks, leaving only empty packing cases. There isn't a thing in this column that we care to save."

Kelton stared, amazed. "But—but why are you doing this?"

Jimmy Christopher laughed sharply. "To decoy the Purple Troops away from those supply trains on the old Missouri Pacific

Line. If I figured things correctly, this column should be attacked at just about this time. And while they're busy capturing empty trucks and spiked guns, we'll be retaliating by capturing— or attempting to capture—those ten supply trains!"

Kelton whistled. "What a stunt! By God, Operator 5, I see it now." Kelton's face abruptly darkened. "But what about those engineers that are building the pontoons; and what about the men on the trucks? They'll be wiped out, won't they?"

Operator 5 nodded soberly. "Yes. Frank Ames here, and the five hundred men who were attached to this column, have volunteered for a service that amounts to suicide. They're going to wait for the attack, and bear the brunt of it. They'll fight as long as they can, to keep the Purple Troops occupied while we attack the supply trains."

"I see," Kelton said, almost under his breath.

Jimmy Christopher turned from the pilot, and faced Frank Ames.

"Frank," he said with a catch in his voice, "I wish to God I could stay here with you. In a short while, you and these men are going to die. You'll have the whole might of the Central Empire battalions down on you like a thunderbolt. And I'll be safely out of it. I had no right to ask anything like this of you—"

Frank Ames' face was calm, but his eyes were shining with

the light of martyrdom. "You didn't ask it, Operator 5. It was my own idea. And the men all volunteered. We're glad to die this way, if it'll help the country. Hundreds of thousands of Americans have perished in the last eight months since the Purple Emperor first set foot on American territory. Many of those Americans died for no good purpose. We, at least, shall not die in vain. If you succeed in capturing those supply trains, and in getting the stuff across to our defense force in the Rockies, it'll be worth many times five hundred lives."

Still Operator 5 made no move. He stood there at the side of the road, and his gaze traveled up and down the long column which was moving past them toward the rapidly growing span of pontoon bridges across the river. His voice was thick with emotion as he spoke.

"I—I can't leave you like this, Frank. I feel like a murderer. Suppose I fail—it'll mean that I've thrown away the lives of five hundred brave men—"

"No, no, Operator 5!" Ames broke in. "Forget about that. Don't think about failure. You can't fail. Now quick—get going. Get into Kelton's plane with Tim Donovan. The pontoons are almost finished, and the enemy will probably attack at any minute. Get going!"

He put out his hand, and Jimmy Christopher took it in a warm, strong clasp. "I'll—get going, Frank. I swear to you, Frank, I won't fail. I won't let you die in vain!"

For a long minute the two stood with hands clasped. Frank Ames's shoulders were thrown well back, and he held his chin high, with a smile of ineffable bravery. The slanting, golden shaft of light from the setting sun illumined his face, revealing a strange expression of crusader fanaticism.

He murmured: *"We, who are about to die, salute you, Operator 5!"* His grip tightened for an instant, then he immediately released Jimmy Christopher's hand. "Go quickly, now!"

Without another word, Jimmy Christopher turned on his heel, strode quickly across the field toward the waiting plane. Kelton, the aviator, followed him. Tim Donovan hesitated a second, while he struggled with a lump in his throat. Then he blurted out: "So long, Frank," and turned and ran swiftly after Jimmy Christopher.

Frank Ames stood still, not moving a muscle, while the plane with Kelton, Operator 5 and Tim Donovan whirred into a roar of motion, and rose gracefully from the field, then merged with the gathering dusk to the north.

CHAPTER 2
DEATH PLAYS DECOY

DOWN BY the river bank, the American engineers were just tying in the last links of the four pontoon bridges spanning the stream. There had once been a bridge here, but it had been destroyed in a pitched battle between retreating American defense forces and the Central Empire troops, some four months earlier. The bridge had never been rebuilt, and the surrounding country had lain fallow and untended while the ruthless march of the Purple Empire progressed westward.

Further east, the impressive memorial to John Brown lay

in a welter of ruins. Here, around the Arkansas River, the tide of battle had laid waste fertile wheat fields and walnut groves, and had destroyed acre upon acre of gushing oil land. The city of Emporia lay in pitiful wreckage of brick and steel; and not a soul walked its once busy streets. A blanket of snow hid from the sight of man the dreadful scars that had been inflicted upon the fertile earth by the powerful machines of war. For the first time in four months men were once more attempting to cross the Arkansas River at this point.

Frank Ames stood at the river bank, watching for a signal from the engineers at the other end that the pontoons were completed. Behind him, the long line of trucks waited, ready to cross. The men in those trucks knew that battery upon battery of enemy guns was trained upon them, ready to unleash a hail of thundering steel that would tear the life from their bodies and crush their bones into pulp. Yet their hands were steady upon the wheels of those trucks, and their eyes were fixed grimly ahead. They had deliberately dedicated themselves to death, setting themselves up as living decoys; and now they waited only for the word of command from Frank Ames, which would set their trucks in motion across those four pontoon bridges.

They knew very well that they would never be allowed to cross the river—that their bodies would float, bloated and stiffening in the ice-caked stream of the Arkansas, battered by continuous shell-fire of the enemy. Yet they were willing and anxious to go on with the suicidal adventure, for there was not a man among them but felt that Operator 5 would make good use of this sacrifice of theirs. It was a stirring testimonial to their faith in Jimmy

Christopher, secure in the knowledge that he would exact from the enemy payment at least to equal the value of each man's life—or himself die in the attempt. In all the annals of history there is no record that any military leader ever commanded such faith from his men.

Now the last links of the pontoons connected the bridges

Another shell struck the pontoon bridge directly in front
of Ames' truck. "Jump! Quick!" he shouted.

with the farther shore, and the workmen ran swiftly back across
the river, moving down the road to mount the driverless trucks
further back in the column.

Ames waited until the last man had returned and taken his
position in one of the trucks. Then he threw a swift glance toward
the ridge to the north, and drew a whistle from his pocket. He

blew three sharp blasts upon it, and mounted to the running board of the first truck.

"Forward!" he ordered the driver. The truck shivered as its motor turned over, and the heavy tires crunched into the hard snow. Slowly the vehicle rumbled forward, moved out upon the northernmost of the four bridges. Behind it, the other trucks spread out from the road, each taking one of the other spans. Ties clicked under the wheels as the trucks rolled over them.

Frank Ames clung to the running board, his eyes glued anxiously upon the ridge to the north. They were half way across now, and behind them, other trucks were swinging on to the bridges. Far back, he could see the long line of the caravan crawling slowly forward. Swift, phantasmagorical thoughts flooded his brain.

Would this sacrifice be a service to the country, or were they throwing away their lives in vain? Ames was young, and he had much to live for. But he had seen his country trodden under the foot of the ruthless conqueror, he had seen the dead bodies of countless Americans littering the streets of ruined cities and scarred battle fields. Since the Purple Invasion had begun, life had become cheap in America. All sense of proportion, and of values, had changed. When they had volunteered for this job of decoy, the lives of five hundred men had seemed but a small price to pay if it would help to bring about the capture of the supply trains which the Central Empire was rushing toward the Rocky Mountains. With death imminent, he began to wonder. He turned back to look at the driver of his truck. The man was gripping his wheel tensely, driving slowly, with lips pressed tight together in a hard, desperate line. For a second, the driver's eyes met those of Frank Ames, and each knew what the other was thinking. They were thinking of mothers, of sweethearts, whom they might never see again. These five hundred men had been carefully selected from among many volunteers. They were men who had no wives or children; yet even these had loved ones whose hearts would contract with pain at the news of their death.

Ames shrugged. The die was cast. It was too late to turn back. AS IF in confirmation of that thought, a puff of smoke suddenly appeared on the ridge to the north. It was followed by a second and a third, and then an avalanche of whining, screaming lead and shell descended upon the river. The earth crumbled under the deep-throated reverberations of the big guns, as fire and flame belched from their mouths. Other batteries, farther east, opened up, laying down a deadly barrage upon the long line of trucks waiting in the road to cross on the pontoon bridges. The white-faced, grim-lipped Americans clung to the wheels of their trucks, driving on through that rain of deadly steel. Shells burst in the road, scattering death, disabling trucks, setting fire to gasoline tanks. Pillars of flame lanced up into the night, as men died in agony.

And yet they drove on. The leading truck, with Frank Ames on the running board, pushed forward across the pontoon bridge. The hail of metal screamed overhead, somehow missing the first and second pontoons, but making direct hits in the center of the third and fourth bridges. There trucks, pontoons, and men thrashed in the river in a litter of blood and wreckage.

The enemy battery on the ridge lowered its sights, and the second pontoon was also struck.

The air was filled with the din of thunderous detonation, whining shells, exploding gas tanks, and the shrieks of wounded men. Somehow, by one of the freaks of war, that first pontoon bridge remained unhit. Frank Ames leaned into the cab of his truck, shouted to the driver above the din and the noise of battle. "Faster! Faster! There's a chance we may get across!"

The truck was swinging dizzily as it raced across the flimsy pontoon bridge. The driver threw a wild, hopeless glance at Ames, then nodded and pressed his foot hard down upon the accelerator.

The lumbering truck gathered speed, while the other vehicles on the bridge behind it pushed close in its wake.

Shells were dropping on both sides, making small geysers as they struck the river. Behind the first two trucks, a shell made a direct hit on the pontoon bridge, and the resulting explosion tore it apart, leaving a yawning gap. Now the enemy had the range of this bridge. In a moment they would smash it out of existence from one bank to the other.

The two trucks were within fifty yards of the opposite shore when another shell struck the pontoon bridge directly in front of Ames' truck. The driver stepped hard on the brakes, and the truck slewed over to the right, with a yawning gap in the bridge directly ahead of it. The truck skidded on the pontoons, and the front right wheel left the bridge. As the big truck teetered on the verge of falling, Ames shouted: "Jump! Quick!"

He motioned wildly to the driver of the truck behind, and

leaped in a wide dive into the river. His own driver followed him, just as the truck slewed over to one side, crashed into the river. Both Ames and his own driver were clear of the falling truck, and they lashed out with swift strokes, swimming toward the opposite shore. Behind them, the driver of the other truck had also deserted his wheel and plunged into the water. The three men swam desperately for shore.

The shells from the enemy battery were dropping with ruthless precision along the length of that pontoon bridge. Before the swimmers reached the shore, there was nothing left of the bridge but a mass of floating wreckage. All four of the pontoons were destroyed, and most of the Americans were marooned on the farther shore.

Ames and the two drivers reached the river bank, climbed wearily up the side. They had escaped death almost by a miracle, and they stood there, their clothes dripping, looking at each other with dull, uncomprehending glances. When they had started over that pontoon, they had never expected to cross it alive. Now as if by divine intervention, these three stood here, still breathing, still whole.

Frank Ames turned and led the way swiftly up the sloping bank toward a thick wood that ran down almost to the shore. They slipped in behind the cover of the bare, snow-crowned trees, and looked through the gathering dusk across the river toward the farther shore, where their comrades on the road were dying under the merciless enemy barrage.

Ames said dully, his voice hardly audible above the din of the bombardment: "They ought to leave the trucks and take cover. My God, why don't they take cover?"

The enemy barrage had moved back from the river, and was now concentrating the entire force of its destructive energies upon the column of trucks. Tall spirals of flame were rising from stricken gasoline tanks, and here and there Ames could see some of the drivers running for cover.

Suddenly the barrage ceased with the abruptness that had accompanied its inception. The flame and thunder of the distant guns melted into silence, with only a few desultory echoes rolling back from the hills. And as if that had been a signal, rank upon rank of enemy infantry came charging out from behind the hills at the double-quick, closing in upon the road from both directions. No one seemed to pay attention to Frank Ames and the two chauffeurs who had escaped to the farther bank. Silently, grimly, they watched in utter helplessness while their comrades were cut down, slaughtered. And then they saw the Central Empire troops hurrying toward the trucks, to see what they had captured.

Frank Ames laughed harshly. "They're in for a little disappointment! Wait till they see those spiked guns, and the empty ammunition cases!"

He swung around to the two drivers. "Come on, boys." He closed his eyes hard, pressed the palm of his hand against them, as if trying to wipe out the sight they had just witnessed—the sight of hundreds of their friends and comrades being butchered by the Central Empire troops. "We should be dead right at this minute, with those boys on the other side of the river. We're living on borrowed time now. Let's make the most of it."

And while the bewildered officers of the Central Empire examined the useless guns and the empty cases in the decoy caravan of trucks, Frank Ames and his two companions stole silently westward....

CHAPTER 3
THE PRAIRIE ARMY

T HE NOISE of the grim fire which was destroying the American caravan of trucks was clearly audible to Jimmy Christopher, Tim Donovan and Kelton in the plane that was swiftly winging northward. They had passed over the low hills behind which the Central Empire divisions were concentrated, and they had seen those massed troops ready to launch their attack upon the doomed column. Then the sudden thunderous outburst of artillery had crashed at their eardrums above the noise of the plane's motor.

Tim Donovan, in the rear cockpit of the three-seated pursuit plane, bit his lower lip, and the lad's eye filled with tears of helplessness at the thought of those Americans who were being blasted to death at the crossing of the Arkansas River.

In front of him, Jimmy Christopher sat staring grimly

forward, his face a taut mask. Kelton, the pilot, glanced backward nervously over his shoulder several times.

Jimmy Christopher adjusted the inter-cockpit telephone set, and spoke into it harshly: "I know how you feel, Kelton. I feel just as bad. But we've got to keep going. Even if we turned back, we couldn't be of any help to those boys. God save their souls!"

Kelton was gripped by emotion. Two or three times his lips moved as he started to speak, then he thought better of it, and remained silent. Gradually, as the distance between them and the Arkansas River increased, the volume of the artillery fire grew less and less. Suddenly it ceased altogether. All three of them were thinking the same thing—had any of those Americans been able to survive the drum-fire? And if so, how many would escape the charge of the Purple Division?

No more words were exchanged among them as they flew steadily northward. Below, they could see the road crowded with motorized infantry, moving steadily southward. These were troops that had been drawn away from the northern part of Missouri to aid in the attack upon the American column of trucks. Thus far, Operator 5's plan seemed to be favored by Lady Luck. The Central Empire was apparently determined to smash that column, and was concentrating all its military force on that sector.

Darkness set in soon, and Kelton was forced to resort to his instruments, flying blind in the night.

Jimmy addressed him again, speaking through the inter-cockpit telephone: "What is our contact with the enemy supply trains, Kelton?"

"We're in direct contact with them," the pilot replied slowly. "Your friend, Miss Diane Elliot, is hidden on board the first train, with a two-way radio set. Some of the boys stole into the railroad yard at St. Louis, and installed the set. They smuggled her on board, and she's been keeping us advised of their progress."

Jimmy Christopher frowned. "Diane Elliot? On board that train? I thought one of the men was going to take that assignment—"

"That's true, Operator 5, but at the last minute the man who was to take the assignment was spotted in the street in St. Louis by a patrol of Central Empire troops, and he was shot down. Miss Elliot was the only one around who could operate the radio set, so she volunteered."

Jimmy Christopher lapsed into silence. Tim Donavon, sitting behind him, stared in mute sympathy at his broad back. The lad knew very well what was in the mind and heart of Operator 5. For Diane Elliot was Jimmy Christopher's fiancée. More than that, she was the girl who had shared his perils and his adventures all through the trying months of the Purple Invasion. JIMMY WOULD have like to place Diane in a gilded cage somewhere, to preserve her safely from the dangers to which she constantly exposed herself. But Diane Elliot had a mind of her own.

Before the invasion of the Central Empire's goose-stepping troops, she had had a career of her own, as well. Star reporter for the Amalgamated Press, Diane had often aided Operator 5 in delicate intelligence work. When the Purple Emperor's mighty forces had first set foot in the United States, Diane Elliot had been the foremost among those of the writing craft to defy the Emperor of the Central Empire. She had been condemned to death and had barely escaped with the daring assistance of Jimmy Christopher and Tim Donovan.

From then on, Diane Elliot had fought unstintingly by Operator 5's side throughout the arduous campaign. Many other American women had taken weapons, and there were even hundreds of them serving in the front lines of the American Defense Forces in the Rocky Mountains at this time. Her risk was no greater than that of these other women, but Operator 5's heart contracted at the thought that he might one day be forced to look upon her white, dead body. Yet he refrained from urging her to avoid risks. Perhaps he might not have loved her as much if she had been the type to seek a sheltered life.

Jimmy Christopher's eyes glowed softly as he looked out into the night toward the northeast, where he knew the thundering supply trains of the Central Empire were even now roaring westward along the old Missouri Pacific line, with Diane secreted somewhere aboard, risking imminent detection while she kept contact by radio with the American conspirators.

His thoughts flew swiftly over the plans he had laid for this daring undertaking upon which he was embarking tonight. Weeks ago, word had come through from patriot spies in the East that this huge shipment of guns and munitions had arrived in New York from the Skoda Works in Europe. Once those guns reached the Purple armies at the Rocky Mountains, the

American Defense Force would inevitably be driven back into the Pacific Ocean.

News of the ten supply trains had come just at the time when Operator 5 had engineered a brilliant *coup* at Pittsburgh, in the heart of the Occupied Territory.* That *coup* had accomplished two purposes; it had destroyed the great steel plants of the Pittsburgh district, and it had also enabled Jimmy Christopher and the selected group of desperate Americans whom he led to capture a store of guns and supplies. But the guns that Opera-

---

* AUTHOR's NOTE: The brilliant *coup* will be recalled by all those who have followed the history of the Purple Invasion as related in these chronicles. Operator 5 had led a determined band of Americans right across the country, through the Occupied Territory, and had, by a bold stroke, seized the barely completed fortifications erected by order of Emperor Rudolph I, on the heights overlooking the city of Pittsburgh. At the same time he led an attack upon the steel plants where the Purple conquerors were forcing American captives to labor at the task of forging guns which would be used to smash the American defenses at the Rockies. That attack was completely successful, and hundreds of captive American toilers, together with their wives and children, were freed and conveyed in safety to the fortified heights. But then the mighty forces of the Central Empire converged upon those heights, besieging the imprisoned patriots. Operator 5 had been forced to order the destruction of the huge, newly constructed Maximilian Dam, across the Ohio, flooding the countryside, and destroying thousands of Purple troopers. He had then led the Americans out in safety, commandeering trucks and cars to convey the captured guns to the coast. The story of this attack may be read in the previous chronicle, entitled "Siege of the Thousand Patriots."

tor 5 captured at Pittsburgh faded into insignificance beside the reports of the specifications of the huge howitzers now being rushed across the country from the Skoda Works.

Jimmy Christopher saw clearly that the only way to preserve the last American stronghold of liberty was to prevent those ten supply trains from reaching the Rockies. So he had planned daringly, risking everything on a single action. Now, as Kelton flew north, he could look down and see the results of his planning. They were not far from the old Missouri Pacific line, and here, directly below them, he could see the flare of campfires. THROUGH THE inter-cockpit telephone he ordered Kelton to dip low.

"Give them the signal!" Kelton nodded, and at the same time took a Very pistol from the side pocket of the cockpit. He held the Very gun far out over the side of the plane, bracing his arm against the slipstream, and fired it. A red streamer of light, ending in a brilliant star, flared from the signal gun. Kelton then fired a second gun, which produced a white star. At once the encampment below became alive with men.

Behind the campfires, Jimmy Christopher could see groups of tethered horses. This was the encampment of a body of Canadian cavalry which Operator 5 had led down from across the border only a few weeks before.* Hidden here in a narrow valley,

---

* AUTHOR'S NOTE: As is well known to those familiar with this period in American history, the Canadian Lancers played an important role in the Purple Invasion. Canada was the first to be conquered by the Central Empire, but the indomitable spirit of the Canadians had been far from

the only chance of their being discovered was by some stray Central Empire plane which might pass; and even such a plane might mistake them for Purple troops, and not report their presence.

The plane under Kelton's skillful guidance circled low, twice, while Operator 5 peered down at a cleared circle around which the Canadians had grouped themselves. In that circle, a cavalryman had lain down flat on his back, and he was signaling up to the plane with semaphore flags.

Jimmy said to Kelton: "Circle them again. I want to get that message."

Kelton nodded, and obeyed, and Jimmy Christopher's quick eye caught the message the cavalryman was conveying by means of the semaphore: *We are ready, Operator 5!*"

Jimmy smiled in the darkness, and said to Kelton: "Okay. I got it."

Kelton dipped the plane's wings twice in token that the message had been received, then continued on the way north. They flew over desolated fields and deserted roads, and Jimmy Christopher was gratified to see that there were no more Central

---

crushed. Sir John Batten had secretly gathered this troop of cavalry, and had marched down to volunteer to serve under Operator 5. They had contacted Jimmy Christopher, and their valor helped to carry the day at Pittsburgh as related in the "Siege of the Thousand Patriots." Unfortunately, Sir John Batten was wounded at a previous engagement, and the command of the Canadian Lancers devolved upon Operator 5. He intended to use them in the present campaign, as will soon be seen.

Empire troops in evidence. Apparently they had all been moved hurriedly toward the Arkansas River to support General von Kurtz in the attack on the American decoy column.

Three miles to the northwest of the Canadian cavalry encampment was the track of the Missouri Pacific line. Much damage had been done to this road in the eight months of the Purple Invasion. A dozen fierce engagements had been fought between St. Louis and Kansas City, and the retreating Americans had been forced to destroy mile upon mile of the line. But other captured Americans had been put to work reconstructing the road, using the latest type of rail-laying devices. The road had been completely rebuilt, and now served as the main artery of supply for the Central Empire Armies in the west.

Tim Donovan was eagerly watching the dark terrain below as they flew over it. His bright young eyes studied everything with youthful inquisitiveness. He plugged in his telephone, spoke into the mouthpiece: "Gee, Jimmy, look at that construction train down there! They're laying track—and they look like Americans, with a few Central Empire soldiers guarding them!"

Kelton had swung the plane westward, following the railroad, and Tim was pointing down at a brightly illuminated scene of nocturnal activity. One of the great track-laying construction trains was being operated by a large crew, and as the plane approached, it could be seen that they were building a sort of spur line leading away at an angle of forty-five degrees from the main line. Perhaps a half-mile away, another construction train could also be seen, moving to meet the first one. The numerous flares down there seemed to indicate that the workers below were in no fear of being discovered.

"If we're going to attack the supply trains, Jimmy," Tim Donovan said worriedly into the telephone, "how will we get past those guards after we capture them? This is right on the road to Kansas City, and we'll have to pass right here."

Jimmy Christopher chuckled. "Those guards are our own men, dressed in Central Empire uniforms, Tim. That construction is going on at my orders!"

KELTON, WHO had been listening in on his phone, whistled. "I thought it was kind of funny, Operator 5. I've seen them working here for almost two weeks, every time I passed. A couple of times, I flew very low, and the American captives didn't seem to be very sad. They looked pretty cheerful. I wondered why the guards seemed so careless, too. There, you can see them now, walking right in among the workers, and helping them on the construction train. What's the idea of laying that track, Operator 5? It just seems to run around in a semicircle, and come back into the main line on the other side of Kansas City."

"I get it!" Tim Donovan exclaimed. "When we capture the supply trains, we run them around this spur, and then back into the Rock Island Line, on the other side of Kansas City. In that way, we avoid the garrison of Purple troops in K.C. Right, Jimmy?"

Operator 5 had been busy releasing two Very gun signals similar to those which Kelton had discharged to signal the Canadians. Kelton circled over the construction train, straining his eyes for a replying signal from the ground below, but he could detect none.

"They're not answering you, Operator 5," he said as he circled for a fourth time. "Can anything be wrong—"

"Oh yes, they are!" Jimmy Christopher assured him. "Take a look at the locomotive of the construction train!"

He said nothing further, but busied himself writing down a series of dots and dashes on a pad he had taken from his pocket. His eyes were fixed upon the locomotive as he wrote.

Kelton frowned in puzzlement, and looked again.

"See it?" Tim Donovan asked.

Kelton shook his head. "All I see is puff after puff of steam coming from the whistle of the locomotive—"

"Those are the signals!" Tim Donovan told him triumphantly. "Don't you see, it's in Morse code—longs and shorts. If our motors weren't making such a racket up here, we'd be able to hear the darn thing tooting!"

"Of course!" Kelton exclaimed, disgustedly. "Why didn't I notice it myself?"

Abruptly, the jerking puffs of steam ceased, and in a moment the locomotive, which had come to a halt at the approach of the plane, resumed its slow course, moving forward to meet the second construction train, which was working its way in the opposite direction from the Rock Island line. As soon as the two construction trains could meet, there would be finished a new spur, skirting Kansas City, and linking the Missouri Pacific with the Rock Island.

Jimmy Christopher held up the sheet of paper upon which he had taken down the Morse code message transmitted by the locomotive.

Tim Donovan was grinning. He said into the mouthpiece: "I guess that's the first time in history that anyone ever sent Morse code by a locomotive stack! If anyone knows of a better one than that, I'd like to hear about it."

The lad leaned over in his cockpit to read the message over Operator 5's shoulder. Both of them could read Morse code almost as fluently as they could read written English. Jimmy Christopher had trained the boy thoroughly, and there had been many an occasion in the adventurous careers of the two, when that ability to read code quickly had saved the day for them.

The message was as follows: *"Spur line will be finished within two hours. All other arrangements complete. Civilians flocking in from all points to volunteer. Good luck to you, Jimmy!"*

It was signed: *"Slips McGuire."*

As the plane circled for a last time over the construction gang, Jimmy Christopher, peering down over the side, saw the familiar, lean face of the man who had sent the message. Slips McGuire was leaning out of the cab of the locomotive, waving a dirty rag up at them. Though they were too far up for him to be sure, Jimmy could have sworn that there was a grin of pure happiness on McGuire's face.

SLIPS McGUIRE was the undersized, wizened little man whom Operator 5 had met some time ago, under tragic circumstances. McGuire's fingers were not those of a locomotive engineer. They were long, flexible, nimble. And at one time, before he had met Jimmy Christopher, McGuire had been a member of the light-fingered gentry who make their living out of the pockets of unsuspecting travelers in the subways of New York. Circumstances rather than inclination had sent the wizened little man into that occupation; and Operator 5, recognizing Slips McGuire's latent qualities, had given him a chance to get out of the sordid life of petty crime into which he had fallen.

Since then, McGuire had fully justified Operator 5's faith in him. He practiced his old profession now in the service of his country, and he had several times purloined documents from the pockets of enemy officers—documents which had been of inestimable importance to the Intelligence Service. As a reward for the signal services he had rendered, Jimmy Christopher had literally forced Z-7, the Chief of American Intelligence, to appoint him as a regular agent. Now he worked in perfect harmony, in the small band of devoted Americans who followed Operator 5. Jimmy Christopher had felt the utmost confidence in placing in Slips McGuire's hands the task of carrying out this plan for seizing the Central Empire supply trains.

He returned McGuire's salutation, then said into the inter-cockpit telephone: "All right, Kelton. Turn around and fly us back along the main line. Land in that field just outside of Sedalia. I'll take active charge now."

In a few minutes Kelton had brought the plane down at the place Jimmy had mentioned. Sedalia had once been an important junction town on the Missouri Pacific. Now it was nothing but a blackened mass of ruins. Months ago the Purple troops of Marshal Kremer had swept over this part of the country, destroying everything in its path. Big guns had battered town after town into the ground, and Sedalia had suffered with the others.

Civilians had been driven from their homes, to seek shelter in the surrounding countryside, to try to live precariously on what little could be gleaned from the ravished land. Americans had taken refuge in huts, in out-of-the-way farmhouses, in caverns and in abandoned mines. Throughout the country, there were millions of men and women hiding in such spots, preferring to die of slow starvation and of illness and cold, rather than come into the populated districts and bend the knee to the conquerors.

If the Purple Empire finally succeeded in subjugating the entire country, these people would eventually be hunted down, tortured and killed as had so many of their friends and relatives. But at present, Marshal Kremer could not muster enough men to probe the vastness of the American countryside for stray fugitives. Temporarily, these hardy patriots might live in comparative safety from discovery, while they faced the rigorous hardships of winter in almost uninhabitable quarters.

It was these people whom Operator 5 planned to use tonight in his daring undertaking. Runners had been spreading through the outlying districts for weeks now, advising the fugitives that they should hold themselves in readiness. And they were overjoyed at the opportunity to strike back at the ruthless victors.

So, when the plane landed at the edge of this field, which had once been a thriving commercial airport, shadowy figures moved out of the darkness toward them.

Old farmers, crotchety with rheumatism, swinging upon their shoulders antiquated muskets which had seen service in the early days of American colonization of the West; youths, still in their teens, too young to serve with the American Defense Forces in the Rockies, but not too young to join enthusiastically in a plot to strike a shrewd blow at the enemy; women, many of them the wives and daughters of Americans who had died in battle—all these had flocked from miles around to volunteer to serve under Operator 5.

The field was alive with eager, teeming humanity. There was little discipline among them, and they were hungry, blue with cold, ill-clad. But every one of them, not excepting the women, carried some sort of weapon, even if it was only a long carving knife, salvaged with the silver out of the family cupboard when they had originally fled before the advancing Purple Armies.

AS THE pursuit ship glided to a stop between the twin rows of flares that had been set down to facilitate their landing, Jimmy Christopher gazed with a sense of satisfaction and thankfulness at the sea of upturned faces surging about them. Also, mingled with his feelings there was a great humility within his breast, at the thought that these hundreds of men and women were eager and willing to entrust their lives to his leadership. He still could not rid his mind of the thought of Frank Ames and those other men back at the Arkansas River who had sacrificed themselves under the enemy's guns so that he could carry out this operation.

He, Jimmy Christopher, once only a number in the records

of the Intelligence Service, was now the focus of the hopes of millions of Americans throughout the land; and he swore fiercely to himself as he descended from the plane that he would not betray the confidence of these people. Far away, in the Rocky Mountains, the American Defense Forces under Z-7 were hanging on desperately to their almost untenable positions, hanging on under the concentrated drumfire of all the mighty Central Empire artillery. And they were hoping that Operator 5 would in some way be able to stop these greater, more powerful guns from being brought up to support the ones already hurling fiery destruction into their trenches.

He must not—he *would not*—fail!

In the forefront of the American volunteers, there strode a middle-aged man in the uniform of a high ranking officer of the American army. Instead of the regulation headgear, however, he wore a wide sombrero, while a huge six-shooter hung low in a holster along his right leg. This was Hank Sheridan,* who

---

* AUTHOR'S NOTE: It will be recalled that Hank Sheridan, uncouth and unlettered citizen of a typical Western mining town, had fiercely resisted the advance of the enemy in the early days of the Purple Invasion, when the Central Empire troops, drunk with victory and slaughter, were marching almost unopposed across the country. With the aid of Operator 5, Sheridan had been able to recruit enough men to stop the Central Empire for a short time; and at Snyder Pass he had inflicted upon them the first defeat since setting foot in the United States. The Battle of Snyder Pass had made Hank Sheridan virtually a national hero, and had metamorphosed him in one day from a small-town mayor to the leader of a powerful force of Americans

had once been nothing more than the rough-and-ready mayor of a small Western mining town, but who had risen during the Purple Invasion to the post of commander of a whole army corps of Americans operating in the prairie states. His presence here at this time indicated what importance the American High Command placed upon the success of Operator 5's plans tonight.

Hank Sheridan clasped Jimmy Christopher's hand warmly, and squeezed hard.

"Well, young feller," he said with his characteristic nasal drawl, "how come you're late? You was expected a half hour ago!"

"I flew down the line," Jimmy explained, "to take a last look at the construction crews. Slips McGuire is almost finished with the spur line. He says he needs two hours more. The Canadian Lancers are holed up in a canyon ten miles from here, and are all set."

They walked across the field through the crowd of Americans who parted before them. Low cheers went up from the hundreds of throats crowding around. Less than a mile from this field were the tracks of the Missouri Pacific, where armed guards of the Central Empire kept constant watch to hold the line clear for the thundering supply trains that were shortly due to pass. From here they could see the lights of the enemy barracks, which had been erected among the ruins of Sedalia. But here, on this field,

operating in Montana and the Dakotas. The thrilling story of the Battle of Snyder Pass was recounted in full in the novel entitled: "Liberty's Death Battalions."

there were dozens of flares, casting a weird, flickering light up into the heavens.

Jimmy frowned. "We don't want the Purple officers to get wind of anything going on here. Why all the lights—"

Hank Sheridan chuckled. "We don't have to worry none, Operator 5. We got outposts strung all along the road from Sedalia. In case the officers at the barracks should wonder what's going on here and send to investigate, their patrol would never return. But they won't get suspicious. They can't imagine the Americans having the guts to congregate like this. They probably think it's a battalion of their own troops. And besides, they haven't got enough men left to do us any harm. They've just got a skeleton garrison in the barracks. You decoyed the main body of their men away to the Arkansas River. It'll take 'em two days to get back."

Jimmy nodded, and motioned for Kelton and Tim Donovan to follow them into the small shack which they had approached, at the far end of the field.

"We got a radio in there," Sheridan told him, "an' we been gettin' steady reports from your girl, Diane Elliot. She's on the train, you know—"

"Yes, I know," Jimmy interrupted. "And I'm worried. Emperor Rudolph has sworn to have her flayed alive if she's ever caught. He hates her almost as much as he hates me. She shouldn't take such risks."

The Americans were crowding in close behind them, and just before entering the shack, Sheridan said: "Why don't you talk to them, Operator 5? They've come from far and wide because you sent out a call. The least you can do is tell 'em what you want 'em for. I haven't let slip what's in your mind—you never can tell, there might be just one traitor among 'em. But I reckon it's safe to tell 'em now. I got the field entirely surrounded by trusty men, and if anyone tried to sneak out now, he'd be spotted."

"Okay," Jimmy said. He stepped up onto the small, rickety porch of the shack, and faced the eager, upturned faces. His eyes filmed for a moment as he noted the eager looks of confidence and trust that were directed toward him.

"Men and women," he said in a voice so low that they had to strain to hear him. "Two weeks ago, I sent word that I would want volunteers for a desperate undertaking. And I see that you have generously answered my call. You are here, armed with whatever you can find, and apparently ready for anything— though you don't even know what I wanted you for." His voice broke. "I—can't tell you how deeply I feel—"

"Forget it, Operator 5," a husky voice in the throng broke in. "We'd follow you anywhere. If you don't want to spring it, you keep quiet. Tell us when you're ready."

"Thank you," Jimmy said. "I think I can tell you now. There are ten enemy supply trains coming along the Missouri Pacific. They're due in Sedalia in a couple of hours. *We're going to attack and capture those trains!*"

INSTEAD OF exclamations of surprise, enthusiastic shouts greeted his announcement. These people knew very well what Jimmy Christopher planned to do; and Jimmy had suspected that they knew. It had not been his idea to keep the information from them. He was not in fear of spies as Hank Sheridan was. Hank had been living for eight months now in the atmosphere of military operations, where it had been necessary to protect themselves against danger of espionage. Several spies had been detected and hanged—usually natives of the Central Empire who had immigrated to America only shortly before the invasion, expressly for the purpose of serving as spies. But here, among the backwoods people, among the men and women who had fled to the hardships of a rigorous winter in the open rather than remain under the yoke of Emperor Rudolph, Jimmy Christopher knew there would be no room for spies or traitors. These people would quickly have learned if there were any disloyal ones among them.

As for their knowledge of his plans, they could not help having a good idea of what he proposed to do. Many of them knew that the Canadian Lancers were hidden near by; many of them were aware of the activity that had been going on along the railroad right-of-way, where the spur was being built, for their relatives and friends were working on those construction gangs, and a good number of them had aided in stealing the rails from the warehouse and in capturing the two construction trains which Slips McGuire was using. As for news of the supply trains, there was little that they did not hear of what was going on throughout the occupied territory, by means of that mysterious grapevine telegraph that grows wherever there are oppressed peoples.

"We're with you, Operator 5!" they shouted. "Just give us a chance!"

Jimmy smiled at them. "No women will be allowed to partic-

41

ipate," he announced. "Men only.
Those—"

He was interrupted by cries of
protestation from the feminine
portion of the crowd. "That's not fair,
Operator 5. We want a chance too!"

Jimmy started to shake his head in the negative, when a big,
raw-boned farm woman in a tan sunbonnet pushed through to
the front. She was clad in a divided skirt, a man's boots, and a
lumber jacket, and she carried a pitchfork across her shoulder.
Her face was deeply tanned by the sun, and her hands were big,
rough from work on the farm.

"You can't keep us out of this, Operator 5," she called out, in
a voice that carried into the night above the murmurings of the
crowd. "My name is Mamie Sandvik, and my husband and my
three boys are all killed by the Purple Armies. I want a chance to
get even for them. There are plenty more women here who have
lost everybody they love, and it ain't fair not to give us a chance.
We're strong. We've worked hard all our lives, and we can fight
as good as any men. Please, Operator 5—" she stretched forth
her free hand in a gesture of pleading—"give us a chance!"

Jimmy Christopher gulped, and swallowed a lump in his
throat. Mamie Sandvik's story was that of thousands of American women all over the country. They had lost husbands, fathers,
sons in the cruel war. They had nothing left to live for now,
except the burning desire to pay back the Purple Emperor for
the wrecking of their homes and their happiness.

Mamie Sandvik, honest, stolid, plodding, had perhaps never

before uttered anything so eloquent of her feelings as those words she had just spoken. They came from deep within her consciousness, and were a definite expression of the misery of bereavement that welled within her capacious bosom.

"I—I'm sorry, Mamie," Jimmy Christopher said thickly. "I—hadn't thought of that—of how you felt about it. I—promise you—you shall have your chance!"

A slow smile spread over Mamie Sandvik's homely features. "God bless you, Operator 5," she said, "for your understanding!"

Hank Sheridan, who was standing beside Jimmy, stirred uncomfortably, and grumbled: "Damn these women! Why can't they stay out of it!" But it was apparent that his gruffness was only a cover for the emotion he felt. He furtively wiped the back of his hand across his eyes, then drew a huge handkerchief and ostentatiously blew his nose. Kelton, the aviator, was also moved, and Tim Donovan was frankly weeping. The lad was thinking of the mother he had never known.

TIM HAD been left an orphan in New York when he was four years old. He had grown into his teens in the hard school of the New York streets. But the sight of the bare emotion in Mamie Sandvik's face now caused faint memories to stir within the boy's consciousness, and released the floodgates of feeling. This boy, who had never known what it meant to be fondled by a devoted mother, now realized abruptly the meaning of maternal love.

He sidled closer to Operator 5, and Jimmy put an arm about his shoulders. Just then the door of the shack opened, and an American in the uniform of the Signal Corps came out. He saluted Hank Sheridan, and said: "I've got Miss Elliot on the radio, talking from the enemy supply train, sir. Do you want to talk to her?"

Sheridan's eyes twinkled. "No, Riggs, but I know someone who does. Go in there and take it away, Operator 5. It's *your* girl!"

Riggs grinned. "Better hurry, Operator 5. Miss Elliot says she hasn't got much time. They're going through the train now, looking for stowaways. She'll have to ditch the radio in a few minutes, and hide."

Jimmy waited for no second invitation. He waved to the crowd, and hurried inside. The shack had been crudely fitted out as a division headquarters office. Two men sat at desks working at rackety typewriters. They were copying a string of orders which Operator 5 had previously outlined, to be dispatched to undercover workers in other sections of the country, through which the supply trains would have to pass after they had captured them. A large map tacked to one wall showed the route of the Missouri Pacific, the Rock Island and other lines serving the West. Colored pins indicated the positions of the enemy troops along these railroads, as far as was known from reports. Other pins showed the hourly-changing position of the American Defense Forces under Z-7 in the Rockies.

There were two radio sets in the room. One was in use, by a man who kept in constant communication with Z-7 and with Slips McGuire at the spur line. The other radio stood beside it, with the earphones hanging to the ground.

Riggs, who had followed Jimmy into the room, indicated the second radio. "She's on that one, Operator 5."

Jimmy nodded, fairly leaped across the room, and donned the earphones. "Diane!" he said into the speaker. "How are you, Di?"

"Jimmy!" Diane Elliot's voice was pitched low as it came over the air. "I'm so glad you're safe. I—I was worried—"

"Never mind about me!" Jimmy said harshly. "What about you? Don't you know that Rudolph has posted a reward for your capture? The devil has some special torture waiting for you. You should never have taken the chance, Di!"

"Some one had to cover the train, Jimmy, and I know how to operate—"

"All right, there's no use arguing about it now, Di. But try to be careful, for my sake. I think I'd go mad if they caught you. It's bad enough that Nan and Mac are prisoners, while I'm tied up here, helpless—"*

"I know, Jimmy." Diane's voice was suddenly full of deep

---

* AUTHOR'S NOTE: Nan Christopher, Operator 5's beautiful, spirited twin sister, had been captured recently in New York, while on a secret mission in company with the Canadian sergeant of Mounted Police, Aloysius MacTavish. Both of them had been sentenced to a painful and humiliating death, to be staged as a spectacle upon the occasion of the formal coronation of Rudolph I as Emperor of America. The coronation had been postponed until the day when the American Defense Forces in the Rockies would surrender and Rudolph would become unquestioned master of the country. In the meantime, Nan and MacTavish languished in filthy, noisome cells, awaiting the day of their ordeal, wondering whether they were forgotten by their friends. The details of their adventures in New York, leading up to their capture, were related in a previous issue. The complete story of their

sympathy. "But some of the boys in New York are working out a plan to help them escape—"

"Never mind that now, Di. Let me have your report." Jimmy Christopher's face was grim. Always now, while he worked feverishly at a thousand tasks in the service of his country, there was in the back of his mind the knowledge that his beloved twin sister, Nan, was a prisoner of the enemy, sentenced to death. A dozen times in the past few weeks he had almost yielded to the temptation to leave everything and hurry to New York to attempt her release. But it was impossible. Everywhere around him he saw examples of self-sacrifice, of bereavement bravely born. Who was he to put personal matters above the duty he owed his country?

So he buried his pain deep within himself, and carried on.

Diane's voice became crisp and businesslike as she hurried into her report. "I'm on board Ordnance Train Number One. They've hooked this Pullman car on, and Colonel Henschel, the Commandant of all the trains, has made it his headquarters. I'm in Compartment B, which is being used as a storeroom. Colonel Henschel is occupying Compartment A, right next door, and the boys in St. Louis installed a dictograph, so that I can overhear everything that goes on in there. I'm safe till some one comes to the storeroom."

"Be careful," Jimmy said.

"We're traveling at about forty miles an hour, and I just heard

imprisonment, and of the coronation of Rudolph, will be told in a forth-coming novel.

some one report to Colonel Henschel that we should arrive at Sedalia in about an hour and a half. The ten trains are maintaining an equal distance of a quarter mile between each, and Colonel Henschel has arranged a system of signaling to the trains behind by leaving colored lanterns on the right of way. There are four hundred Purple troops on this train, so you'd better have plenty of men when you attack. If you capture this one, the other trains will be easy, because they're carrying only skeleton crews. Colonel Henschel doesn't anticipate any trouble. He can't imagine the American's attempting anything against them in the heart of the Occupied Territory—"

Suddenly Diane's voice ended in a quick gasp.

"Di!" he shouted into the microphone. "What is it—"

"Jimmy! I'm caught—"

That was all she said. The air went dead. Not another sound came from the receiving set. Jimmy Christopher's knuckles whitened as he clutched the microphone, called into it, "Di! Di! What is it?"

There was no answer.

Slowly, heavily, Operator 5 removed the earphones from his head. There was an immense emptiness in his chest. He knew only too well what had happened.

Diane had hung on to the last minute; and that minute had been one too long. She had been discovered. She was a captive of this Colonel Henschel, whom she had mentioned over the radio—if she had not already been killed while defending herself. At that, it might be better for her to die while resisting capture, by gun or bayonet, rather than to be preserved for the tender mercies of the Emperor, Rudolph I.

Jimmy Christopher raised haggard eyes to Tim Donovan and Hank Sheridan. Neither of them asked him any questions. They had both listened closely, and they knew as well as he did what Diane's sudden silence meant.

Hank Sheridan put a hand on Jimmy's shoulder, pressed hard. Tim Donovan's hands were clenched at his sides, and the boy was biting his lips. There were four or five American sub-officers in the room, and they all watched Jimmy Christopher. Each of them knew what Diane's capture meant to her and to Operator 5. There was a slim chance that she might be kept on the train.

There were other possibilities, however, which were more likely. For instance, it was more likely that Colonel Henschel would telegraph back to New York at once to notify Rudolph of his prize; and Rudolph would surely order Diane sent back at once. The train would stop, and she would be transferred to a car or plane.

TIM DONOVAN

If they waited here to attack the trains, they would probably not find her aboard—even if they were successful.

THESE THINGS were working swiftly through the mind of Hank Sheridan as well as of everybody else in the room. They watched Jimmy Christopher rise slowly from his chair. He seemed to have grown years older in the space of minutes. He avoided meeting the gaze of Hank Sheridan or Tim Donovan.

For a long time there was silence in the room. Then Hank Sheridan cleared his throat. "She—she's been captured, of course?"

Jimmy nodded.

"Well—" Hank glanced around self-consciously—"suppose we go to meet the trains instead of waiting here. There are fifty freight cars in the yards over at Sedalia. We could load all our men on them, and go meet them half way. Maybe we'd get them before they send Diane back—"

"No!" Jimmy Christopher's voice, hoarse with emotion, caught him up short. "You know very well, Hank, that we'd never stand a chance of capturing those trains if we did that. We've got a barricade erected here, and the Canadian cavalry is ready. And we've got to get those trains off this main line and on to the spur that Slips is building. If we had to do fifty miles on the main line after capturing them, the enemy could locate us with their bombing planes, and blast us out of existence. The very success of the plan depends on our disappearing with the trains—throwing them off the trail. No, Hank—" he put a hand on the older man's shoulder—"it's good of you to suggest it, but I'd be a cad and a traitor to accept the suggestion. Neither of us has the right to risk the success of this plan for the sake of any one person. Frank Ames and those boys of his died gallantly at the Arkansas River, to enable us to go ahead with this thing here. What would they say if they could know that I had deliberately thrown away our chances of success, had deliberately wasted the sacrifice of their lives, by trying to save one person—no matter how dear that one person is to me?"

Hank Sheridan lowered his eyes. "I—I guess you're right, Jimmy. But—I know it's hard on you!"

Tim Donovan exclaimed incredulously: "Jimmy! Do you mean to say you're not going to do anything to save Diane? You're going—to leave her to be taken back to New York? Don't you know that Rudolph said he'd have her flayed alive?"

"I'm sorry, Tim. I can't do anything else. Diane will understand."

He turned brusquely away from the boy's accusing glance, and began to issue swift, curt orders. "Riggs! Communicate at once with Major Bowlton, commanding the Canadian Lancers. They are to saddle and ride at once. Have them meet me here in forty minutes. Tell Major Bowlton not to ride the horses too hard; they'll need their wind."

Riggs saluted, said: "Very good, sir," and stepped to the radio.

"Hank!" Jimmy Christopher went on swiftly. "Take these officers outside, and organize the volunteers. Divide them into squadrons, but keep the women separate. Let them think they are going to take an active part in the fight, but actually move them back to a position far enough away so they won't be able to come up in time. Let them make a sixth squadron. Of the five squadrons of men, assign one to attack the barracks when the signal is given. They are not to attempt to take the barracks, but just to keep the enemy there so busy that they won't be able to come to the assistance of the troops on the trains."

Hank Sheridan nodded, his old eyes gleaming with admiration for the sagacious way in which Operator 5 was planning the battle—as well as for the stoicism with which he was repressing every feeling about Diane Elliot, subordinating his personal emotion to the needs of duty.

"And what about the other four squadrons?"

"Two squadrons to the north of the railroad tracks, and two to the south. They are to hide in the brush, out of sight of the trains, and they will not advance until after the cavalry have charged. The idea is to get the troops out of the trains, on to the ground. We'll have only about fifty men at the barricade across the tracks. The enemy will pour out to clean up the barricade, and then we'll charge. Get the idea, Hank?"

"Okay, Jimmy."

"And—Hank."

"Yes, Jimmy?"

"Tell the men, when they board the train, to look out for Diane, will you?"

"Don't worry, Jimmy. I'll tell them."

While the preparations were going forward, Jimmy Christopher slumped down into a chair, and bowed his head. Hank, with the subaltern officers, left the shack, and his stentorian voice could be heard from outside, issuing orders to the volunteers, assigning his officers to their commands. No one was left in the room but the two radio operators, the clerks who were intent on their work, and Tim Donovan.

Tim stepped close to where Jimmy Christopher sat, and leaned down over him. The lad could see that Jimmy's lips were moving, and bending closer, he caught the words: "Diane, dearest Di. Forgive me—for murdering you...."

Choking back the tears, his young face twisted into a mask

of emotional agony, Tim Donovan uttered a hoarse sob, and ran headlong from the room.

CHAPTER 4
THE FOX SCENTS A TRAP

RUMBLING WESTWARD in the night, some fifty miles east of Sedalia, Central Empire Ordnance Train Number One resembled some huge Frankenstein of iron, dedicated to death and destruction. Two locomotives hauled the long train, spurting clouds of smoke and cinders into the air. Behind the locomotives rolled flatcar after flatcar, upon each of which were mounted huge new guns.

Long, graceful, deadly guns, each capable of hurling a ton of destructive shrapnel, poked their silent fingers up into the sky from behind steel armor that sheltered the crews. Squat, stubby, vicious-looking howitzers which could send high explosive whining over a mountain squatted upon other cars like fat Buddhas thirsting for slaughter. Those flatcars had been specially constructed to accommodate these guns; and the guns themselves were far in advance, in point of construction and effectiveness, of anything that had yet been used in modern warfare.

If those guns should ever reach the front lines at the Rocky Mountains, no human force could hope to stand against them.

And scattered Americans, watching the passing trains from nearby fields, looked on with bitterness in their hearts, knowing that these supplies would sound the death knell of the last remnants of American liberty when they began their deep-

throated roar on the Western Front.
Those watchers did not know of the
plans of Operator 5 at Sedalia; but
there were other Americans ensconced
in little dugouts at a respectful distance
from the right-of-way, who turned
eagerly to telegraph instruments and
clicked out the news of the passing of
Number One.

These men had been installed in their pill-boxes at the orders
of Operator 5, for the purpose of keeping him informed of
the exact location of the enemy at all times, thus serving as a
check upon whoever was posted at the radio in Ordnance Train
Number One—and also, in case that person should have failed
to gain access to the radio.

The trains themselves moved forward upon singing rails,
piloted by picked Central Empire engineers. The engineers did
not hesitate as they drove their huge charges westward, nor did
they fear hidden bombs or other obstructions upon the tracks.
For the locomotives were equipped with photo-electric rays
that lanced invisibly far out ahead of the speeding engines. If
those rays were to encounter an obstruction of any sort upon
the tracks, they would immediately cause a red bulb to come to
life in the cab of the locomotive, conveying warning to the engineer in plenty of time for him to apply his air brakes. It was the
knowledge of the existence of these photo-electric rays which
had deterred the Americans in the East from attempting to blow
up the trains with dynamite charges.

Flatcar after flatcar rumbled past the ruins of small towns along the railroad line. Eight months ago, those small towns had been thriving commercial and manufacturing communities and farming centers. Now, no lights shone from warm buildings where happy families had once gathered after the day's work. Here and there a structure still stood with gaping holes in the walls; but for the most part, the buildings lay in black ruins, serving as the tombstones of the once prosperous towns.

Now and then the powerful headlights of the locomotive, swinging around a curve, would illumine the shadowy figure of a fugitive American, come back to hunt among the ruins of his home for some family heirloom that had been overlooked in the panicky flight from the Central Empire bombardment; or that same shadowy figure might be searching among piles of fallen brick and timber for some sign of the bodies of his loved ones, buried under the wreckage.

And once, a tattered, frozen, bedraggled figure, standing beside the charred timbers of a hut, arose and shook his fist wildly after the thundering train, screaming out mad imprecations. Then, after the train had passed, he knelt, sobbing wretchedly, beside the pitiful figure of a dead woman, who clutched the still form of a lifeless child fiercely to her breast, even in death. Those two had not perished in the bombardment. Only the day before the mother had carried her child back to the hut from their refuge in the fields. The cold had grown bitter, and the child was sick. The mother had dared to return, in the hope that the four walls of the hut would afford the child shelter while the mother tended its illness.

But a Central Empire patrol, passing that way, had seen the candle light in the hut. Those raucous, bawdy troopers, following the example set by their Imperial master, had amused themselves with the mother all through the night, forcing her to do their wishes in the hope of saving her baby. Then, in the morning one of the troopers had callously thrust a bayonet through the woman's breast, while another had impaled the baby. And so the father found them.

Throughout the land such things were daily occurrences. Was it any wonder, then, that the women at Sedalia were ready and eager to fight side by side with their men?

ORDNANCE TRAIN Number One thundered through the night, cutting down the miles toward Sedalia. Behind it rolled nine more long, serpentine-like trains, with their big guns sheltered behind armor of steel, or with car after car of ammunition for those monsters. And in Compartment B of the Pullman car which was hitched on to Number One, a tense, dramatic scene was taking place. Diane Elliot, twisted about in her seat before the radio, was facing the burly Central Empire colonel who had just stepped into the room, revolver in hand.

Outside, wind shrieked past the window as the train raced across the dark countryside and cinders from the locomotive far ahead beat against the pane. But neither Diane nor the colonel paid attention to anything but each other.

The colonel's small eyes were glittering, and his red tongue licked at thick lips. He bowed with mock courtesy. "This is indeed a surprise, Madame—to find a so beautiful lady on our

"You will tell me quickly what you are doing here—"

supply train. Why do you hide your beauty in the storeroom? Why not come out?"

Diane Elliot's soft chestnut hair set off the beautiful oval of her clear-complexioned face. One hand pressed at her white throat, while the other was clenched tensely against the open bunk upon which the radio had been set up. On the floor there were a dozen cases of champagne, and boxes containing tins of caviar and other delicacies. Each of those boxes was marked: *"For personal delivery to Marshal Kremer at Staff Headquarters."*

There had been an imperial seal upon the door of the compartment, for these delicacies were being sent as a special gift from His Imperial Majesty, Rudolph I, to Marshal Kremer. The purpose of the gift was to signify the Emperor's pleasure at the victorious outcome of the campaign of conquest. At St. Louis, Diane and the Americans who aided her had removed the seal, replacing it with a forged copy after Diane was installed within, with the radio. They had been able to do this while the train lay in the St. Louis yards, with only a sentry on duty.

Diane had been confident that she would not be interrupted, for she knew the respect which the Imperial seal instilled in the officers of the Purple Army. She could not understand, therefore, what had prompted Colonel Henschel to violate the seal and enter this compartment.

Henschel guessed what she was thinking. "Your scheme was very clever, Miss Elliot—"

Diane started. "You—know who I am?"

"But of course. Your picture has been circulated throughout the Occupied Territory. The Emperor has set a large reward upon your head. But as I was saying—your scheme was clever. You might have remained here undetected for the remainder of the trip, for no one would have dared to break the Imperial Seal without good reason. I would not have thought of looking here for anyone, had I not discovered a very interesting little instrument in my compartment."

Diane was watching him carefully.

"Exactly. And my electrician traced the wires. They led directly here. Now perhaps you will tell me, Miss Elliot, why you are concealed on the train."

Diane had regained control of herself. "Can't you guess, Herr Colonel?"

"No. I cannot imagine what earthly reason you could have, unless an attack were being planned against the train. And such a thing is unthinkable. The Americans would not dare!"

He took a step closer. "You will tell me quickly what you are doing here—"

Diane swung around swiftly, snatched at the automatic pistol which she had kept beside the radio on the bunk. Henschel had taken her by surprise, and she had been too stunned to reach for it before. Now, as her hand darted out for the weapon, Henschel stepped in swiftly, and seized her wrist, twisted it viciously. Diane gasped with the sudden pain, and struck at him with her right fist. The blow caught Henschel on the side of the jaw, but he only grunted, and increased his pressure on Diane's arm.

He yanked her up out of the chair, snarling: "You little spitfire!" And then, holstering his revolver, he brought his open left hand down across her face in a cruel smashing blow. The sound of that blow snapped like the crack of a whip. Diane's head was jerked back, and a wide red splotch appeared on her cheek. At the same time she gasped with the agony in her arm, which Henschel was twisting more viciously. Her body was forced sideways under the leverage of that painful grip, and the Colonel laughed cruelly. It seemed to Diane that the bone would snap at any instant.

Desperately she kicked out at her captor, and the toe of her shoe caught him in the shin. Henschel yelled with pain, but did not let go his grip. Instead he tightened it, and raised a fist to smash down into her face.

The train lurched, and Diane was thrown backward against the bunk, falling over the radio. It was that lurch which saved her from having her nose smashed by Henschel's huge knotted fist. He lost his balance, fell forward toward her, and the blow missed her face, landed on her left shoulder, sending excruciating pains down her left side.

She lashed out again and again with her right foot, and once more she caught Henschel in the leg, just below the knee. This time she had the support of the bunk behind her, and there was force to the kick. Henschel howled with the pain, and tears came to his eyes. Abruptly he relaxed his grip on her arm, and danced around the small compartment, yelling, on one foot.

Quickly, Diane reached over for the automatic she had dropped, but Henschel, his small eyes burning with insane rage, swung a huge fist that smashed into the side of her head with a sickening thud. Diane was hurled back on to the bunk, and lay there, still.

HENSCHEL LAUGHED harshly, still rubbing his leg where he had been kicked. He reached out, gripped the unconscious girl by the hair, and dragged her off the bunk, dropped her to the floor. Then he stood over her, drew back his foot, and kicked her deliberately in the body, again and again. Each time his boot thudded into her soft flesh, he grunted with animal satisfaction. Then he turned and strode out into the corridor, where a guard stood at attention.

"You will stand before that door," he ordered the trooper. "No one must enter. If the girl regains consciousness and attempts to leave, you will give her a few gentle jabs with your bayonet." He winked at the guard. "Enough to be very painful, you understand, but not enough to injure her severely. We must save her for the Emperor."

The guard saluted stiffly, and moved over to stand in the corridor, facing the open door of the compartment. The man's bovine eyes rested upon the unconscious figure of Diane, traveled over the soft, rounded curves of her body. He licked his lips.

Colonel Henschel strode forward through the swaying car, and entered his own compartment. An orderly arose and stood at attention.

"Signal the engineer to stop at the next military station!" Henschel commanded crisply. "I wish to send a wireless to His Imperial Majesty. We have splendid news for him!"

Twenty minutes later, the train stopped for water at a military station along the right of way. These stations were erected at twenty-mile intervals along all railroads which were used by the Central Empire for transporting military supplies. They consisted of concrete block-houses, generally garrisoned by an officer and five men, who were charged with patrolling the line for ten miles in either direction. To each garrison was assigned one baby tank which operated under the command of the garrison officer, and which was used in subduing any isolated revolts which might break out in the surrounding territory. In this way Rudolph was able to enforce his power over the vast reaches of conquered country.

Vast numbers of these baby tanks had been brought over from European armament plants, and they were really the backbone of the Central Empire's Army of Occupation. For Rudolph's effective troops numbered not more than four million, and these were in themselves inadequate to police a hostile country of one hundred and twenty million souls. But Rudolph was able to keep three and a half million of his goose-stepping troops in service at the Front, because the half million, by using the tanks, were able to keep the conquered territory in subjugation.

Colonel Henschel descended from Ordnance Train Number One, and gave orders to signal the trains behind to slow down. He entered the concrete block house, and ordered his message sent out to Imperial Headquarters in New York. He smacked his lips as he dictated the news:

> To His Imperial Majesty,
>
> Rudolph I, Emperor of Europe and Asia:
>
> Your humble and loyal servant, Colonel Johann Henschel, kisses your hand and begs to report that he has just captured the woman, Diane Elliot, known to be the fiancée of Operator

5. She is now under guard, and your obedient servant awaits the Imperial Command as to what disposition he shall make of the prisoner.

Signed,
Colonel Johann Henschel,
Commanding C.E. Ordnance Train
Number One.

The young lieutenant in charge of the garrison looked at Henschel enviously. "You are indeed fortunate, Herr Colonel. His Imperial Majesty has promised that the man who captures either Operator 5 or the Elliot girl shall be made governor of one of the conquered provinces!"

Henschel nodded. "A title of nobility goes with the reward. I shall probably be made a Baron of the Empire!"

The reply to his wireless came back almost with the speed of lightning, testifying to the efficiency at Imperial Headquarters. Henschel frowned as he read the flimsy strip handed to him by the wireless operator:

To Colonel Henschel, Commanding

C.E. Ordnance Train Number One:

Why do you not tell in detail how the Elliot girl was captured? Where was she found? Reply at once.

Flexner.

The signature at the bottom of the curt message was that of the Prime Minister to His Imperial Majesty, Rudolph I. Baron Julian Flexner was the ideal adviser for a man like the Emperor. If Rudolph was savage and sadistic, temperamental and unstable,

Flexner was suave, controlled, calculating and shrewd. No man wielded more power in the Central Empire than Baron Julian Flexner—with the exception of Rudolph himself.

COLONEL HENSCHEL paled as he read the telegram. Like most of the army officers, he hated Baron Flexner, resenting the fact that he must take orders from a civilian. But he realized also that he should have given more details in his message. While the young lieutenant snickered behind his back at his discomfiture, Henschel dictated a reply:

> Elliot girl was aboard my train, hidden in Compartment B, which was used as storage room for His Imperial Majesty's gifts to Rudolph. Forged seal was placed on her door, and a dictograph was installed in my office. I traced the dictograph to Compartment B, and broke the seal, recognizing it as a forgery. I found the Elliot girl working a radio sending and receiving set, and captured her after a bitter struggle. She is at present unconscious. Am awaiting orders.

His answer came back quickly:

> Fool! Why did you not question her as to her reason for being on the train? She did not go aboard merely to overhear what you were saying to your subordinate officers. There must be some plot afoot to attack the Ordnance Trains. Proceed with caution henceforth. Detach one of your locomotives and send it ahead as a scout. Keep within signaling distance of your scout locomotive at all times.
>
> Have the Elliot girl transferred at once to the tank attached

to garrison. Tank is to proceed at once to Kansas City, then westward to Denver. His Imperial Majesty is flying to Denver in the morning, and will question her personally. I will speak to His Imperial Majesty about a suitable reward for you.

Flexner.

Henschel spat in disgust. "Fool, he calls me! He will speak to His Majesty about a suitable reward for me!" The colonel shook his finger in the young lieutenant's face. "Mark you Lieutenant Meister, Flexner, will go too far one of these days!"

"Perhaps he will, Herr Colonel," Lieutenant Meister replied. "But until then, we must obey him. Shall I have the girl removed from the train?"

"Do so," Henschel grumbled. He left to give orders for detaching one of the locomotives and sending it on ahead as a scout. While Diane Elliot, still unconscious, was being carried into the tank, the scout locomotive started out down the track, with a complement of twenty troopers and a signalman aboard.

Henschel stood moodily alongside the tank, watching two of the troopers loading Diane's limp figure into the small armored steel tank.

Flexner's biting message still rankled in the colonel's bosom. He considered that the Prime Minister was depriving him of his just dues in ordering him to transfer his captive to the tank. Flexner might even fail to inform the Emperor of the name of the officer who had captured her, or the wily Baron might minimize Henschel's part in the exploit. He felt that he was being treated unjustly, but he dared not disobey Flexner's order.

Suddenly, an idea occurred to him. His thick lips twisted into

a cunning smile. He stepped quickly
to the side of Lieutenant Meister, who
was directing the fueling of the tank for
its long trip to Denver.

"How fast can this tank travel?" he
demanded.

"It is one of the newest models,"
Meister told him. "It can make better
than fifty miles an hour, and it can cross
country that an ordinary automobile could never negotiate."

"H'm," Henschel mused. "My trains are moving at only forty
to fifty miles an hour. Good. I shall take command of the tank,
Lieutenant Meister. You will remain here in charge of the garrison. I will take the three men of the tank's crew with me, and will
keep pace with the trains. In that way, I will be able to turn over
the Elliot girl personally to His Majesty in Denver!"

Meister was doubtful. "But can you leave your trains, Herr
Colonel—"

"That is for me to judge," Henschel told him coldly. "I am
obeying Baron Flexner's order to the letter. He said nothing as
to my remaining with the trains. I am in immediate command
of the entire convoy, and if I choose to ride in the tank, that is
within my discretion. If an attack should take place, I could join
the trains at once. And besides, I would have the Elliot girl as
a hostage."

Meister shrugged. "As you choose, Herr Colonel. The tank is
at your disposal." Henschel hurried back to the train, and issued
instructions to his aide, Captain von Steig. "You will take charge

of the convoy, von Steig. I am taking the tank with the prisoner. Should anything arise that makes it necessary to communicate with me, have the engineer sound six blasts of his whistle." Von Steig saluted.

In a few moments, Ordnance Train Number One rumbled off in the wake of the scout locomotive. Behind Train Number One rumbled the other trains of the long convoy, each keeping its distance. Henschel watched them all pass, then he clamored into the baby tank, stepped over the body of Diane Elliot, who was lying prone on the floor, and gave the order to start.

The tank rolled away, its two small guns poking out into the night. Henschel stared down at Diane, who was just beginning to stir. He felt of his shins, which were still sore where she had kicked him.

"Little spitfire!" he muttered savagely, and smashed his foot into her ribs in another vicious kick.

Diane stirred, and groaned.

Henschel snarled: "I shall become a Baron of the Empire through you, little spitfire—and I shall be present at your execution when you are flayed alive. Each strip of flesh that is torn from your white body will be another rope by which I shall climb to greatness in the service of the Emperor!"

The crew of the tank eyed him with misgiving. They could not hear his words above the rumbling of the tank, but they thought he was acting somewhat strangely....

CHAPTER 5
BLOODY BARRICADE

A T T H E railroad yards outside of Sedalia, everything was quiet except for the occasional shifting of a freight car as the yard crews worked to clear the main line for the convoy of ordnance trains.

At the barracks, sentries made their rounds, while the officers dined inside. None was aware that only a mile or so to the west, the spur line was being finished to carry the trains around Kansas City. None was aware of the dark masses of men who stole through the cold winter night toward the barracks, or of the other groups that lay hidden in the brush on either side of the railroad tracks. If any of the yard crews, or any of the sentries, had taken the trouble to walk down those tracks about a quarter of a mile beyond the Sedalia yards, he would have halted in astonishment at sight of the thick tree trunks that were lying across the main line, forming as effective a barricade as could be imagined. Those tree trunks had been hauled onto the tracks by sheer manpower, and piled up so that they would be visible to the engineer even before the photo-electric rays warned him of the obstruction.

Jimmy Christopher had calculated to a nicety just where the train should come to a stop after the engineer applied his airbrakes. That spot was alongside a cleared field that ran out into a wooded thicket. Behind that thicket the battalion of Canadian Lancers sat tensely upon their restive horses, waiting for the word that would send them galloping to the charge.

Operator 5's plans were carefully laid, and he himself sat upon a horse at the head of the column of cavalry. He was determined to lead that charge himself.

Thus far, he had allowed many men to sacrifice themselves for the sake of this plan. Now that it was nearing completion and his efforts were to be put to the test, he had turned a deaf ear to the pleas of Hank Sheridan, of Tim Donovan, and of Major Bowlton, all of whom had entreated him to remain in the headquarters shack while the attack was made.

Something seemed to have gone out of him since he made the decision to leave Diane Elliot to her fate, and to wait here for the trains. His face seemed to be set in granite as he replied in the same way to all arguments:

"Gentlemen, my mind is made up. Everybody has had a crack at death—even Diane. Now it's my turn."

"But it's suicide, Operator 5!" Major Bowlton protested. "When the enemy troops pile off the train, they'll be armed with submachine guns and rifles. It's true that a cavalry charge is the ideal thing to break them up, but it's also true that whoever leads that charge is certain to be killed in the first volley."

"That's right, Major," Jimmy Christopher said dully.

Bowlton exclaimed eagerly: "Then you'll let me lead the charge instead—"

"On the contrary, Major, I'm going to lead it."

Hank Sheridan groaned. "Don't be a damned fool, Jimmy. You're feeling all cut up about Diane. You think you'll be responsible if she's tortured and executed by Rudolph. But how do you know they've got her? How do you know she didn't escape?

And besides, you owe it to the country not to thrust yourself into danger.

"Do you think your work will be done even if we capture the ordnance trains? It's just begun. There's the job of getting those trains clear across the country, through the enemy troops. There's only one man who can do a stunt like that, Jimmy, and that man is you."

"I'm sorry, Hank. I'm going to lead the charge. Back at the Arkansas, I let Frank Ames and his boys throw away their lives; just now, I deliberately left Diane in the lurch, left her to the mercy of Rudolph; my own sister is a prisoner in New York, together with Sergeant MacTavish. I've sacrificed everybody I held dear, for the sake of the country. Perhaps it was worth it. Right now, I feel that I'm a murderer. I'm going to pay up. You can't deprive me of that right!"

Hank threw up his hands, sent a hopeless glance at Tim Donovan and Major Bowlton, as if to say: "I can't do anything with him. Maybe you can."

Major Bowlton said shrewdly: "After all, Operator 5, the Lancers are a Canadian outfit. I'm their commanding officer, succeeding Sir John Batten. Don't you think a Canadian outfit should be led by its commanding officer, and not by an American?"

Jimmy Christopher shook his head stubbornly. "I don't want to appear rude, Major Bowlton, but I want to remind you that Sir John Batten turned over the command of the Lancers to me when he was wounded and carried off the field of battle—"

Whatever further arguments the others might have advanced

were to remain unsaid. For at that moment a man came running from the headquarters shack, skirting the edge of the wood. He was heading straight for Jimmy Christopher, and Hank Sheridan exclaimed: "The ordnance train must be near. They've got word from our observers!"

THE MESSENGER reached Operator 5, clinging breathlessly to the pommel of his horse for a moment, then reported breathlessly: "We've just got word that an enemy locomotive is ten miles away, heading this way. The ordnance train itself is about a mile behind it. If the locomotive reaches the barricade first, the trains behind will be warned of the ambush. What'll we do, Operator 5?"

Hank Sheridan exclaimed: "Good God! There goes our whole plan! We'll never take them by surprise—"

Jimmy Christopher frowned. "Ten miles away? That means it should reach here within fifteen minutes. They must suspect an ambush after having found Diane."

"But what'll we do, damn it?" Hank Sheridan demanded. "Should we move up along the road and attack the train when it stops—"

"No. Fifteen minutes is a lot of time." He swung around to Major Bowlton. "Ride down to the thicket, and get a hundred of the men. Bring them to the barricade—quickly!"

He did not wait to see if he was obeyed, but spurred his own horse across the field toward the track. The men at the barricade saw him coming, and advanced to meet him. Jimmy flung from his horse almost before it came to a halt, let the reins hang, and shouted to them: "Quick, men! Get to work on those tree trunks. We've got to haul them off the tracks in fifteen minutes!"

The men failed to comprehend for a moment, thinking that the plan for the ambuscade had been changed. Jimmy explained to them swiftly, and they set to work with a will. The ropes they had used to haul the logs on to the track were found once more, and were looped around the top trunk. There were some forty men here, but it took the combined efforts of all of them to move the heavy length of timber. Jimmy Christopher seized one of the ropes, hauled with the rest. Laboriously, they managed to pull it off, clear of the track.

By that time, Major Bowlton came up with a second group of men, and these jumped to work as well. They sweated in the cold night, moving log after log, until only one was left across the track. A locomotive whistle sounded alarmingly near.

Bowlton groaned: "God, we'll never get that last one off in time. Here comes the engine!"

Frantically the men looped the ropes around the last log, then turned and harnessed themselves into the loops at the other ends of the ropes, and dragged, dragged, straining every muscle of their already aching bodies. The log budged slightly. It was the heaviest of the tree trunks, and the sweat was running down the faces of every one of the men. They strained and strained, with the enemy locomotive drawing nearer every moment. They could see it now in the night, hardly a quarter of a mile away. In another half minute it would be close enough so that its photo-electric rays would pick up the obstruction and warn the engineer.

Only the end of the tree trunk was on the track now, but the men were exhausted. Jimmy Christopher pulled with the others, his eyes ever on the swiftly approaching locomotive.

"Come on, boys!" he shouted. "One last pull! One, two, *three!*"

They all heaved mightily, and the great log slid off the rail. The track was clear!

"Get down, everybody!" Jimmy yelled.

They all dropped on their faces to the cold ground, just as the monster of iron roared past them. Now they could see, too, in the distance, the locomotive of the ordnance train, sparks flying from its stack as it rumbled toward them.

Jimmy knew that the men were virtually exhausted, but he pushed them mercilessly.

"All right, everybody!" he shouted. "Get to work. Back on the tracks with those logs!"

The men did not hesitate. They fell to, not sparing themselves. One after another the huge tree trunks were shunted back on to the rails, while the ordnance train raced at them. When the second log was in place, Jimmy Christopher ran to where he had left his horse, followed by Major Bowlton.

He called back to the men: "Get as many of those trunks back on the tracks as you can. Then get behind them!"

With Bowlton alongside, he spurred across the field, and around behind the wood to where the Canadian Lancers waited. Hank Sheridan and Tim Donovan had already left to join the volunteer Americans hidden in the thickets. The mounts of the Canadians were champing at their bits, prancing and restless to go.

THROUGH THE woods Jimmy could see the ordnance train slowing down as the electric eye notified the engineer that the road was not clear. He would not suspect a barricade now, for he felt secure in the knowledge that the scout locomotive was ahead of him. He would be more apt to think that it was the locomotive itself, slowing down for some reason.

From where they sat their horses they could hear the screech of air brakes being applied, and Jimmy nodded in satisfaction as he watched the train come to a stop almost directly opposite the wood behind which they waited.

The train was now scarcely a hundred yards from the barricade, and by this time the engineer must know that it was not his scout locomotive ahead, but something far different.

As the rumbling of the train died down, Jimmy Christopher raised a whistle to his lips, blew a single shrill blast upon it. That was the signal for which the men behind the log barricade were waiting.

At once a volley of rifle fire burst from behind the barricade, raining upon the front of the locomotive in a steady, clangorous tattoo.

Jimmy Christopher rose in his stirrups to look beyond the train toward the barracks. He could see the flashes of rifle fire there, too. So far, everything was going off according to schedule. The company of Americans assigned to the barracks was launching its attack. They would keep the few troops busy, preventing them from coming to the assistance of the train.

Far behind, they could hear the whistle of Ordnance Train

Number Two, slowing up as its electric eye notified it of danger ahead.

Now Jimmy could see troopers climbing down from the gun cars of Train Number One, many of them carrying machine guns. He could see Central Empire officers forming the troopers into companies, and could see them returning the fire of the Americans behind the barricade. A contingent of troopers moved to the left, into the field, evidently with the intention of taking the ambuscaders in the flank.

This was the moment that Jimmy was waiting for. He raised his saber, shouted: "Forward!"

He spurred his horse ahead, and behind him four hundred sabers rose in the air as the Canadian Lancers moved after him. Major Bowlton rode alongside Operator 5. Hooves drummed on the sod as the cavalry increased its pace, coming out of the wood into the field. As yet they were unnoticed. A few of the Central Empire troopers had remained alongside the train, and were returning the fire of the Americans behind the barricade. But the main body was out in the field, moving swiftly ahead to take them from the left.

An officer glanced around, suddenly stiffened as he glimpsed the ghostly figures of the massed horsemen riding toward them. He waved his sword, shouted a swift order. The troopers swung around, facing the cavalry, and dropped to their knees on the ground, raising machine guns and rifles.

"Now!" shouted Jimmy Christopher. "Charge!"

A wild yell arose from four hundred throats as the troop bent low upon their horses and spurred forward. Rank upon rank of cavalry followed Jimmy Christopher in a thundering charge across the ground, hardened by cold.

The drumming of the horses' hooves sounded a furiously swift undertone to the shouts of the gallant lancers, mingling with the volleying fire from the Central Empire soldiers.

The Purple troops were taken completely by surprise, and their fire became unsteady, irregular. Lead sang overhead, and slugs bit into the ground. Miraculously, Jimmy Christopher rode through the deadly hail. His face set in hard lines, his saber outthrust ahead of him, he seemed to represent to those Central Empire infantrymen the embodiment of some avenging spirit come to exact terrible payment for the tortures and the killings they had inflicted upon American captives.

And now, from the thickets on either side there poured a motley, ragged crowd of shouting volunteer Americans, armed with muskets, scythes, pitchforks and old swords. Behind the men, the American women, who had been segregated by Operator 5's order into a single company, refused to be restrained, and joined in the attack.

The night was filled with the drumming of hooves, the crackling of rifle and machine-gun fire, and the shouts of battling men.

The cavalry charged on, directly into the face of the enemy's fire. Men and horses began to fall among the lancers, but Jimmy Christopher, who seemed to be courting death, rode through it as if he bore a charmed life. Bullets tugged at his clothing, grazed his horse, and churned the ground in front of him. But he rode on.

IT HAS been observed that those men who seem most eager to seek death in battle are spared by the Grim Reaper. The phenomenon has been witnessed in every age, and in every land where man has waged warfare against man. In the trenches of France during the World War, there were men who sought to die for many strange reasons. They would show their heads above the trenches, they would charge machine-gun nests, they would volunteer for suicidal expeditions into No-Man's Land. And it was those men who were usually spared throughout the war, while their very neighbors, who perhaps loved life dearly, found their names engraved on a bullet or a bit of shrapnel. Thus it was tonight with Jimmy Christopher. Major Bowlton had said that to lead this cavalry charge would be suicide. Yet both he and Operator 5 reached the front rank of the enemy unscathed, while men fell behind them. Who can explain these quirks of fate? Who can account for the erratic whim of a bullet that speeds through the air with the velocity of light, blindly striking down whomever it encounters?

Can it be that Death is like some shy beauty, hiding her face from those who seek her? Or is it true that the fate of every man upon this earth is written down beforehand, and that no matter what mad risks he takes, he will not die one minute or one second before his allotted time?

Philosophers from time immemorial have witnessed deeds of bravery and daring, and have pondered upon these questions, without finding an answer. Men have delved deeply into the secrets of life; but who among us can say that he has even scratched the surface of the veil which darkly covers the secrets of Death? Perhaps when we go to our final rendezvous with the shy beauty whom men call Death, we shall at last learn those secrets. Until then we can only surmise.

Jimmy Christopher had often given thought to what lay beyond this life of ours. And now, as he rode fiercely at the head of his thundering cavalry, directly into the hail of gunfire, he was aware of that same adventurous glow of expectancy which the intrepid wanderers of bygone ages must have felt upon approaching some unknown and hitherto uncharted land. He rode eagerly forward, expecting Death to pluck at him at any moment, and feeling almost a joy at the contemplation of it.

Yet no bullet touched him. Ahead, not ten yards away, he could now see the frantically firing Central Empire troopers, kneeling and pumping their rifles, while behind them, other troopers worked desperately at sub machine guns. The wind whipped through his cap as his horse raced headlong at the front ranks of those troopers. He felt himself to be a thunder-bolt, hurling himself at the enemy, and he must truly have been a terrifying figure to them, with the solid phalanx of horsemen behind him, brandishing keen-edged sabers as they leaned far forward over their horses' heads.

That thundering charge was too much for the enemy. The front ranks broke, and turned to stumble away in desperate panic, to get away from the threat of those sabers. And in an instant the cavalry was upon them, cutting and slashing, riding them down, breaking them up.

Central Empire officers yelled to their men to stand and fight. They struck at them. Like mad animals seeking shelter. But it

79

was useless. The panic was among them. Like made animals seeking shelter from the hunters, they brushed aside their officers and fled out of the path of the whirlwind charge. To right and left they scattered, only to be met by the grim, determined volunteer Americans on foot; Americans who for eight long months had harbored a rankling hatred of the cruel invader; Americans who had been compelled to watch brothers, fathers, sons executed before their very eyes; Americans who had come home to find their wives violated and their children murdered; Americans who attacked them fiercely, wildly, with strange, uncouth weapons such as no army had used in modern warfare before—pitchforks that speared them like fish, scythes that swished through the air to sever heads from bodies, and old, outmoded muskets used as clubs to beat down their bayonets and bash in their heads.

The battle broke up into small thrashing groups and man-to-man fights. The shouting and yelling ceased, the tumult died down, and the fighting went on in grim silence, with no quarter asked or given.

Those Purple troopers, accustomed to easy victories through the superior strength of their equipment, were no match for the fierce Americans fighting to avenge loved ones and the sacking of their homes.

It took only a few moments for Jimmy Christopher to understand that the battle was won. He blew his whistle a dozen times, in an attempt to stop the fighting and demand the surrender of the surviving Purple soldiers. But the shrill notes of the whistle received no attention. The embittered Americans paid it no heed. They were too grimly intent on the business in hand.

AND JIMMY CHRISTOPHER could not find it in his heart to blame them, when he remembered the pillaged homes, the execution blocks that had been erected in every captured city, and the fiendish torture devices conceived by the rulers of the Central Empire. He knew how these men felt, for he too had loved ones in the hands of the enemy. Diane....

Diane!

Perhaps she was still on the train!

He spurred his horse through the battle, toward the train. His troops had spread out now, and a close-packed body under Major Bowlton had ridden back to where the other trains of the convoy had slowed up behind Number One. The long line of flatcars, stretching far back into the night, resembled impotent monsters now, no longer dangerous to the American Defense Force. The first step was successful. Now it remained to pilot those guns over mile upon mile of railroad, through enemy territory, to the Rocky Mountains.

Jimmy Christopher found his mind confused as he galloped his horse up the Pullman car at the end of Ordnance Train Number One. Thoughts of Diane mingled with thoughts of the work yet to be done. The sounds of battle still dinned in his ears, but suddenly he knew that all this would be an empty triumph—that even if the Purple Emperor were to be driven from America, it would not reawaken the spark that had died in him when he had heard Diane's voice over the radio: *Jimmy! I'm caught!*

As he spurred through the battle toward this car, he was aware of a dim reluctance to enter it, fearful to discover for certain that Diane was not there. He saw Tim Donovan mounting the cab of the engine, saw the engineer lean down to fire a pistol full in the lad's face, and he saw Tim fire just one split second before the other. He saw the engineer's face disintegrate under Tim's bullet, then watched the boy climb victoriously into the engine.

At another time he would have ridden through the crowd of fighting men to congratulate the boy, to slap him on the back, perhaps to chide him for risking his life in a grown man's task. Now he merely looked, then rode on.

At the Pullman car he dismounted, climbed stolidly into it. A dead trooper lay in the entryway, face down, still clutching his rifle. Jimmy stepped over the man's body, entered the corridor, and went from compartment to compartment, from berth to berth.

The door of Compartment B was still open, and inside, the cases of champagne and caviar were still piled up. His blood raced as he saw the radio on the bunk, the small automatic pistol on the floor which he had once presented to Diane, and which he knew she always carried.

Of Diane herself there was no sign. He felt certain now that she had been taken off the train, sent back to New York, to the tender mercies of Rudolph. And he was conscious of a great emptiness within him.

His feet dragged sluggishly as he made his way through the corridor, stepped once more over the body of the dead trooper, and descended to the ground. His horse stood patiently where he had left it. The battle was over. As he gazed over the field and the right of way of the railroad, he could see no prisoners. The Americans had taken none. The field was dotted with still, unmoving bodies. The cavalry was reforming at the edge of the field, under the orders of Major Bowlton.

Hank Sheridan, in the center of the field, was attempting to organize the volunteer Americans into ranks once more. From the direction of the barracks on the other side of the tracks could be heard the victorious shouts of the Americans who had attacked the garrison. The victory was complete. Yet it tasted bitter to Operator 5.

CHAPTER 6
WHITE FLAG

LISTLESSLY, JIMMY CHRISTOPHER began to cross the field toward Hank Sheridan. There was much to do, and he had little spirit for it.

But suddenly, in the twinkling of an eye, all that was changed.

Operator 5 was startled by a shout that abruptly went up from the Canadian Lancers at the edge of the field. They were pointing toward the automobile road, which approached Sedalia at an angle to the railroad tracks and crossed them. Jimmy's glance followed their pointing fingers, and he stiffened as he saw a small tank rolling to a stop, with the insignia of the Central Empire painted upon its turret.

The tank's guns were silent, and even as he watched, the side of the tank slid open, and an officer stepped out, waving a white handkerchief. Behind the officer came the three members of the tank's crew, carrying between them a limp figure which was impossible to identify in the dark.

At sight of the Central Empire officer and men, the volunteer Americans uttered angry shouts, and would have rushed forward to attack them, regardless of the white flag. But Hank Sheridan restrained them.

The Central Empire officer took several steps away from the tank, and then stopped, as if waiting for some one to approach him from the American forces. Behind the officer, the tank crew had carried their burden around to the front of the tank, where they appeared to be busying themselves in front of the left hand tread, with long coils of rope.

Major Bowlton waved across the field to Operator 5, signifying that the next step was up to him.

Jimmy frowned, and advanced to meet the Purple officer. As he drew near the man, he recognized the insignia of a colonel of ordnance upon the man's epaulets. He stopped ten paces from the other, said in the language of the Central Empire: "What do you wish?"

The officer smiled twistedly. "I am Colonel Johann Henschel, Colonel of Ordnance in the Imperial Army of His Majesty, Rudolph I, Emperor of—"

"Never mind the trimmings, Colonel," Jimmy Christopher said tartly. "Come to the point. Why do you show the white flag, and what do you want? I warn you that we are here in force, and your tank stands no chance against us. If you wish to surrender—"

"That is farthest from my thoughts, sir," Colonel Henschel

returned urbanely. "But before I state my mission, I should like to know with whom I have the honor of parleying. Are you the commanding officer of these Americans?"

"I am Operator 5," Jimmy told him concisely. "I am in command here. You may state your message."

Henschel grinned broadly. "Our meeting could not have been more opportune, Operator 5! I will come to the point quickly. In the name of His Imperial Majesty, Rudolph I, I hereby call upon you to surrender to me these trains which you have just captured, together with all supplies therein contained. I will be merciful, and will not require that your followers surrender themselves; they may lay down their arms and disperse. However, I do demand that you and the officers immediately under your command place yourselves in my custody—"

"Are you crazy?" Jimmy Christopher demanded. "Nobody admires courage in a man more than I do. But your attitude now is mere foolhardiness—"

"Not at all, my dear sir," Henschel said softly. "You think you hold all the cards here, but you are mistaken, Operator 5. *I* hold the *trump card!* Look for yourself!"

He stepped aside, and Jimmy Christopher stiffened, all the blood draining from his face. He felt for an instant as if a powerful drug had been injected into an artery, causing his blood to expand within his veins.

His eyes dilated at sight of Diane Elliot, *tied to the tread of the tank!"*

THE TANK crew had stepped away from the tread, and had quickly reentered the tank. Diane was conscious now, and she rested, helpless in her bonds, facing Jimmy. Her feet were close to the ground, and with the first movement of the tank, the tread would move, carrying her down, under its crushing weight, grinding her bones into pulp. But even with the knowledge of what awaited her, she held her head up defiantly, her little chin raised, her breasts heaving under the ropes.

Jimmy Christopher strove to control his feelings. Upon coming out of the Pullman car, he had thought Diane lost to him forever, had visioned her under the hands of some sadistic executioner, being tortured dreadfully for the delectation of the Purple Emperor. Now, he saw her alive, but his quick mind grasped the implications of the situation immediately.

Once more her fate was to be in his hands. Once more he was to be confronted with the choice of saving the life of Diane Elliot, or of setting aside his duty to his country. He knew very well that every man among those Americans, and among the Canadian Lancers as well, would be willing to have him turn over the captured troop trains to Colonel Henschel if it meant saving Diane's life. And he knew just as well that he could never permit them to do it—even if he had to stand and watch the girl he loved ground to death under the tread of that tank.

Colonel Henschel said bitingly: "I need not speak further, Operator 5. You understand the situation thoroughly. All your men here could not stop that tank from moving forward five feet. Those five feet would be enough to crush your young lady into a writhing mass of flattened flesh and bone. Or—"he leered disgustingly—"we could advance the tank only three feet and crush her body up to the waist. Then you could have the pleasure of holding her in your arms while she lived for a few moments more. Give me your answer, Operator 5!"

Before Jimmy could reply, Diane's clear, cool voice came to him, carrying through the night: "Jimmy! Don't give up! Shoot me, quickly. Kill me, dearest, and then capture the tank!"

Colonel Henschel laughed harshly. "Kill her, Operator 5! Kill the woman you love! Go on! Shoot her!"

Jimmy Christopher stood tense, while the blood raced through his veins. He was immovable, like some mortal of Greek mythology who has suddenly been turned to stone by the act of a god.

Henschel went on: "You may capture the tank later, of course, and you may kill me and my men. But how could that restore the crushed bones of the beautiful lady? They could never be made whole again!"

He raised his hand in signal, and the tank moved forward an inch, almost imperceptibly. But it was enough to force Diane's feet down against the ground. She had to push them forward against the ropes to keep them from being caught under the tread.

She called out chokingly: "Kill me quickly, Jimmy! For God's sake kill me! I love you, Jimmy, and I'll always love you, even in death!"

Operator 5's hand clenched around the butt of the revolver in his holster. He did not answer her, and Henschel thought he was still fighting it out with himself. In reality, he was doing nothing of the kind. Out of the corner of his eye he had noticed Hank Sheridan and a group of Americans steal off the field, and then quietly sink out of sight in the wooded thicket. He knew what they were doing; they were going to crawl around, attack the tank in the hope of surprising the crew while they kept the door open for Henschel's return.

It would take them time to do that, and he must win that time for them—he must stall the colonel in some way. Now his lethargy was gone. There was a slim chance of saving Diane, and all his faculties were bent to the task of assisting Hank and his men to approach the tank undiscovered. If the attack failed, then he knew for certain that he would place a bullet through Diane's heart rather than let her be crushed under the tread. He would never accede to Henschel's demands, and if Henschel had known him better, the colonel would never have offered him the choice.

He would kill Diane, yes, with his own hand. And then, he swore to himself, he would fire one more shot—*into his own brain!*

But there was a chance—such a slim chance—that Hank might succeed. Jimmy Christopher's eyes suddenly became alive, absorbed in the problem before him, and his mind raced ahead. He must make Henschel think he was considering the proposition, must make him wait. He could shoot the colonel, yes. But then he would have to shoot Diane at once to save her from a worse death.

Almost automatically he spoke: "How can I be sure, Colonel Henschel, that you will release Miss Elliot if I comply with your terms?"

Henschel laughed insolently. "I did not say that I would

release her. She will remain a prisoner, together with yourself and your other officers. You will all be taken to Denver, where his Imperial Majesty expects to arrive tomorrow or the next day. I can promise you that you will all be treated with clemency if you surrender. Consider the ordnance trains are of no use to you. You could not transport them to your army in the Rocky Mountains, for you could not even pass Kansas City. Though many of our troops have been moved out of this sector for some sort of operation at the Arkansas River, the garrison at Kansas City is still maintained at its full quota. You could never run these trains through there. On the other hand, if you surrender, your young lady will be spared from being crushed under the tank, and I will pledge my word that you will all receive mercy from the Emperor."

Jimmy knew that Henschel was lying. No officer in the Purple Armies could pass his word as to what the emperor would or would not do. Henschel was merely trying to tempt him into surrendering. After that, he would sing a different tune.

Henschel went on: "Believe me, Operator 5, I am a kind man...."

JIMMY WAS listening to him with one ear only. He was watching out of the corner of his eye, for some sign that Hank and the others had skirted the field, were close to the tank. Out on the field, the Lancers under Bowlton and the American volunteers knew what was taking place, and they remained rooted to their places, in anxious suspense. None of them uttered a word. All eyes were fixed upon Diane Elliot, while they visioned the agony she would endure when the tank passed over her body.

Mamie Sandvik, standing with the other women, muttered to a companion: "How can Operator 5 stand there and watch his girl doomed to die? Why doesn't he surrender? None of us would blame him. If I were in her place, I wouldn't care what my husband did to save me!"

Henschel was saying in a loud voice, so as to be heard by all: "I am by nature a kind man, Operator 5…. I hate the sight of suffering, and I revolt at the thought of inflicting such a punishment as this upon so beautiful a young woman as Miss Elliot. But what would you?" He spread his hands placatingly. "This is war. In the service of my emperor—"

"Don't believe him, Jimmy!" Diane called out. "He's not kind. He's cruel, savage, mean. I'd rather be dead than in his hands—"

Jimmy Christopher tensed. He had seen a little flurry of motion out on the field behind the tank. Hank and his men were stealing up. He could even see one of the Americans behind Hank, with a small black object in his hand. It was a grenade. They intended to fling that grenade into the tank….

Henschel had half-turned and in a moment he would be facing in that direction, could hardly fail to see the stealthy attackers.

Desperately Jimmy Christopher called out to him: "Look here, Henschel. What's to prevent me from taking you prisoner, and holding you in exchange for Miss Elliot?"

Henschel turned back to face him, and the danger was gone. "This will prevent you, Operator 5!" He raised the white handkerchief which he was carrying. "I came to talk with you under the protection of a flag of truce. Under the rules of international warfare, you must permit me to return to the tank, unmolested, before resuming hostilities." He shrugged. "It will, of course, be too bad if Miss Elliot should be the first casualty after hostilities are resumed."

"I don't take that view, Colonel," Jimmy said coldly. "The tying of a defenseless girl to the tread of a tank is not countenanced by any rules of international warfare. Since you have violated them, I feel free to disregard your flag of truce." His hand came up from his holster, holding the revolver centered upon Henschel's chest. *"Put your hands up, Colonel!"*

Henschel stared at him, not finding it possible to believe that he would thus deliberately sacrifice Diane—to have the life crushed out of her body.

"You fool!" he shouted. "If you shoot me, the tank moves forward—"

His words were drowned by the blasting sound of an exploding grenade.

Jimmy Christopher had timed his action well. He had seen Hank and the other Americans close in on the open tank door, had seen one of the men raise his hand to hurl the grenade; and he had drawn his gun at that moment.

A cloud of smoke smeared itself around the tank, for the moment obscuring sight of Diane. The grenade was not powerful enough to blast out the sides of the tank. Exploding inside, it destroyed everything in the interior, but Diane was unharmed.

The Americans and the Lancers uttered wild shouts, and broke into a mad rush toward the tank.

Henschel, under cover of the confusion, attempted to turn and flee. Jimmy leaped after him, seized the towering colonel by the shoulder, and spun him around, sent a hard fist crashing into his mouth. Henschel screamed and clawed at his holster. Jimmy gave him no chance to draw, but sent another right full in his face, felt cartilage smash under the impact of the blow. Henschel backed away, covering his face with his elbow, still clawing at his gun. He had it half out when Jimmy followed in close, brought a hard jab up to the side of his head, then another to the point of his jaw. Henschel gasped as consciousness left him, and sagged to the ground.

Jimmy didn't wait to see if he would rise, but raced across the field toward the tank. The smoke was clearing away, and he could see Hank and the Americans swarming around the tank, while a Central Empire soldier, miraculously alive after the explosion of the grenade, fired at them from an open porthole in the turret. Diane was still tied to the tread, watching the Americans with wide eyes.

Jimmy turned at the sound of his name being gasped out, and saw Tim Donovan racing beside him. The lad leaped down from the locomotive cab, and had caught up with him while he was fighting Henschel. Tim had pulled out a long clasp knife, and had flipped open the blade.

Jimmy reached out, snatched the knife from Tim's hands, and ran in under the very gun-muzzle of the trooper in the tank. The trooper lowered his gun to aim at Jimmy, and simultaneously the explosion of a shot sounded from behind Jimmy's left shoulder. Tim Donovan had stopped short, taken careful aim, and his slug caught the trooper squarely between the eyes.

Jimmy Christopher slashed at the ropes, cutting them away with frantic haste. The last of them fell away, and Diane slumped over, fairly sagged into his arms. She had fainted from the strain.

Jimmy held her tenderly, pressing a long kiss upon her ashen lips, oblivious of the sympathetic glances of Hank Sheridan, Major Bowlton, and the others.

"Darling!" he murmured. "Darling, with you alive, I've got something to live for!"

Diane's soft body quivered in his arms, and she shuddered. Then she opened her eyes, and met his gaze. For a long minute she stared at him emptily, as if not recognizing him. The shadow of terror lay in her face. Then suddenly, her eyes lost their vacant expression, and recognition came into them.

"Jimmy!" she gasped. "For a moment I thought I was still a prisoner of that dreadful Colonel Henschel!" And she began to cry.

Mamie Sandvik came and took her out of Jimmy's arms. "Come along, you little sweet. I'll get you a coat or something, to wear. We'll ride in the Pullman car again—only you won't be a prisoner this time!"

Jimmy watched them climb into the Pullman, together with a number of the other women. Then he swung to Hank Sheridan and Major Bowlton. He seemed to be a new man—as if he had been fed a dose of some revitalizing serum. He issued swift orders, sent men scurrying in every direction, some to remove the barricade from the road, others to the barracks to remove all arms and ammunition, and still others to man the cabs of the locomotives of all the ordnance trains.

Tim Donovan, watching him, grinned slowly. "The old Jimmy is back again. Thank God!" he said fervently.

CHAPTER 7
THE RAGE OF RUDOLPH I

THAT NIGHT, the wires and the airwaves across the country were alive with dismayed reports, angry orders, biting recriminations and drastic punishments.

Word was flashed across to New York that ten ordnance trains had been captured by the Americans under Operator 5, in the heart of the Occupied Territory. At first, neither Baron Flexner nor Emperor Rudolph would believe the news flash that came in from Sedalia, sent by a junior Central Empire Officer who had hidden himself in an unused room of the barracks, thus escaping the vengeance of the Americans. After Jimmy Christopher pulled away with the ten trains, and the last of the volunteer Americans faded into the night, this officer came out of hiding and crept to the radio, managed to get a message through to the station at Jefferson City, which relayed it to St. Louis, thence to Imperial Headquarters at New York.

Baron Julian Flexner, pale and trembling, carried the radio operator's written transcript of the message to Rudolph, who was about to sit down to a late supper with a dozen of his fawning courtiers.

Rudolph frowned at his Prime Minister, waved him away. "Don't bother me, Flexner. Can't you see I'm being entertained? Go away. Nothing can be so important that it won't keep—especially when I'm being entertained!"

He pointed to the source of the entertainment, across the room from his table. The courtiers about laughed loudly.

The entertainment consisted of two American girls, neither more than sixteen or seventeen, who had been caught in the streets after six p.m. A strict curfew law was enforced in every American city in the Occupied Territory, and any Americans found in the streets between the hours of six in the evening and nine in the morning were subject to instant execution without trial.

Occasionally Rudolph chose to amuse himself with some of the prisoners, as with these two girls. They had both been stripped to the waist, the dresses torn ruthlessly from their shoulders, and hanging precariously at the hips.

They stood now, with their faces to the wall, their wrists tied high above their heads so that their toes barely touched the floor. The white, soft skin of their bare backs, glistening under the electric lights, was criss-crossed by ugly red welts. Those welts were caused by the two long cowhide whips with which Rudolph and his courtiers were taking turns at beating them.

"It's a game," Rudolph explained to Flexner, who stood stiffly disapproving. "We throw the dice, you see, and whoever gets the highest number has first chance, and so on. The man who makes them scream loudest is the winner!"

He threw a contemptuous glance at the two girls, whose

bodies were quivering with the pain of the lashings they had already received.

"These two are pretty good. They haven't screamed yet. But they faint too easily. We've had to pour cold water over them three times already, to revive them!"

Flexner frowned. "I am sorry, Sire, but I cannot approve of

RUDOLPH

MAJ. GEN.
VON KURTZ

COLONEL
HENSCHEL

this. I humbly beg to remind you that whenever you have driven these Americans too far, they have invariably revolted. They are not built like our Europeans. It is impossible to cow them. They think more of their liberty than they do of their lives. The news of what you are doing to these two girls will spread in the city tomorrow, and I will have to turn out the guards again, to quell a new revolt."

Rudolph waved aside his argument. "Not this time, Flexner, not this time. With Operator 5's sister in a dungeon here in New York, and with the Elliot woman a prisoner in the West, we have them in the hollow of our hand. Operator 5 will not dare to move against us. And when our ordnance trains reach the Rocky Mountains, we will drive the last of the American troops into the Pacific and set up a really iron rule. They will not dare to breathe, these damned Americans—"

He stopped, noting the distressed look upon Baron Flexner's countenance. "What is it, Flexner? Why do you act like that? What is it?"

Flexner's lips trembled. He started to speak, glanced down at the message in his hand, then clamped his lips shut.

"Come, come, Flexner. I see that you have bad news. What is it—another revolt in the west?"

"Worse than that, Sire. Much worse."

"Well, speak up, man. What is it?"

"Diane Elliot is no longer our prisoner, Sire—"

"What! Did that fool of a colonel allow her to escape? I'll have him shot. I'll have him drawn and quartered—"

"Wait, Sire. That is not all. Perhaps you should read this your-self—"

"Never mind. Tell me what it says. Hurry. What can there be more—"

"Our ordnance trains, Sire. They have disappeared!"

"*What!*"

"A large force of Americans under Operator 5 set a trap for the trains at Sedalia. They captured all ten trains, and annihilated the troops convoying them. Then they drove the trains away."

"Impossible! It couldn't be done, Flexner. It couldn't be done. We have troops and tanks throughout that territory. There were plenty of men on board the ordnance trains. It would have taken a large force—"

"They had a large force, Sire. They also had cavalry. The cavalry charge demoralized our men, and made the victory certain for the Americans."

Rudolph sat back in his chair, twisting his moustache fiercely. "I can't believe it. Where could they have hidden so many men? Where could they have gotten the courage to plan such an attack? And where can they take those trains? Why, Flexner, they'll have to pass through Kansas City. Our garrison there is strong—strong enough to stop an army. They could never get through—"

"Alas, Sire, they did not go through Kansas City."

"They didn't go through Kansas City? Then where did they go? Are they still on the line between Kansas City and St. Louis?"

"No, Sire. The line has been scoured thoroughly. The only thing we found was the scout locomotive which Colonel Henschel sent ahead at my order. The scout traveled fifty miles before it found it was not being followed. It returned along the same line to Sedalia, without encountering the ordnance trains. We found a spur line leading away from the main track at Sedalia, and I have just ordered a locomotive to follow that spur and find where it leads. Perhaps that will give us some hint of where the trains are."

Rudolph clenched his fists in rage. "Damn that Operator 5!" he shouted hoarsely, while his face grew red in an apoplectic fury. "It is he who causes me all this trouble! Is there not a man among my officers who can catch me this Operator 5? I will reward him beyond his wildest dreams!"

"I have high hopes that we will be able to trap him soon, Sire," Flexner said soothingly. "He will slip sooner or later—"

"Bah!" Rudolph spat disgustedly. "You have told me that before. He is still at large."

Suddenly he arose, a figure of towering rage. He glowered at the courtiers: "Get out! Get out, all of you! Leave me alone!"

Terrified, the courtiers backed out, leaving him alone with Flexner, and with the piteous figures of the two unfortunate girls spread-eagled against the wall.

Rudolph leveled a finger at his Prime Minister. "How is it that the garrison at Sedalia was not able to repel this attack? We maintain a large garrison there."

Flexner fidgeted. "True, Sire. But most of the troops were moved to the Arkansas River, to aid in an attack upon an American column of trucks pushing through to the west."

"And they succeeded?"

"Yes, Sire, they succeeded. Unfortunately, they discovered that there was nothing of value in the trucks. The guns had all been spiked, and the ammunition cases were empty. It seems now that the whole column at the Arkansas River was nothing but a hoax on the part of Operator 5, for the express purpose of drawing our troops away from northern Missouri, thus leaving him free to attack the ordnance trains."

"God!" Rudolph exclaimed. "That man is clever. I would give anything to be rid of him. But never mind it now." He glared at the Baron, shook a fist in his face. "You must see to it that those ordnance trains are recovered, and that Operator 5 is captured. I will give you two days to accomplish that. Use all the troops you want. Spread them like a blanket over the sector where those trains might be. Leave no corner unsearched. Those trains must be brought back. Do you understand? Otherwise I shall have a new Prime Minister the day after tomorrow!"

Flexner was pale. "I—understand, Sire."

"Now leave me!"

Flexner bowed himself out of the room.

RUDOLPH, LEFT alone, seemed to be in the throes of a fit, so great was his ungovernable rage. He had been able to control himself more or less while Flexner was in the room. Now he gave free vent to that rage, storming up and down the room, with saliva drooling from his mouth.

For eight months, ever since he had set foot upon the soil of the United States, he had been plagued by the courage and resourcefulness of the man who was known as Operator 5. At every turn he had found himself balked by the foresight and clever planning of Operator 5. With nothing but the broken resources of a half-conquered nation at his disposal, Jimmy Christopher had been able to slow up the advance of the superbly equipped Purple troops, had been able to strike shrewd blows at the Empire, had on more than one occasion made Rudolph appear foolish before his own troops. Rudolph's own cousin, whom the emperor had hoped to carry, had deserted to the American side, attracted by the courage and wit of Operator 5.

That defection of his cousin, the Baroness Anita Monfred, stung Rudolph in his pride as a man.* His hate for Operator 5 was increased a hundredfold, and he promulgated an order to the effect that any man who turned Operator 5 over to him, a captive, would be granted the governorship of a whole province in the Occupied Territory. He had even attempted to bribe civilian Americans, but had not succeeded in finding a single one who would betray Operator 5, no matter what pressure was brought to bear.

---

* AUTHOR'S NOTE: The part which the Baroness Anita Monfred, Rudolph's cousin, played in the Purple Invasion is known to all those who have interested themselves in the little-known sidelights of the history of the period. Several incidents involving her have already been related in previous novels of this series, and forthcoming installments will deal with some further aspects of her activities during these exciting times. For the present it may be said that though she was engaged to Rudolph, with the prospect of becoming Empress of the World upon marrying him, she had given up all that to follow Jimmy Christopher. Though she knew that he loved Diane, and that her love for him must be hopeless, she had left Rudolph and his cruel excesses, and she now lived in San Francisco in the last stronghold of the retreating Americans. But her life was not a happy one, for there was a price upon her head in the territory of the Purple Empire, and the Americans looked upon her with suspicion because of her former associations. She was truly "A Woman Without a Country!"

Rudolph's hatred and disappointment increased, until the name alone of Operator 5 was sufficient to send him into a towering rage. Now he paced up and down the room, a prey to hopeless, intolerable jealousy and hate. His eyes lighted upon the two girls, still shackled to the wall, and his gaze traveled up their bare, tortured backs.

His lips twisted into a sadistic smile. Here was an avenue of escape for his rage, his pent-up emotion.

He snatched up the cowhide whip, strode over to them. The whip whistled through the air, cracked down across the back of the nearest girl, ripping away skin and flesh. Her body stiffened, then shivered convulsively, but she said nothing. Again and again he brought down the heavy lash, then took a step forward, repeated the performance with the other. At last, his arm weary, he stopped, gazing at the bloody bodies of his victims. His eyes were bloodshot, and his lips were flecked with bloody saliva where he had bitten them in the transport of his sadistic orgy.

He stared now at the two semi-conscious girls, and burst into loud, raucous laughter. "Well," he croaked hoarsely, "why don't you say something? Why don't you beg for mercy? Beg, damn you, if you don't want to be flayed alive!"

The girls stirred, and moaned. One of them twisted her head to look at him, and it was evident that she was using the last vestige of her failing strength to speak.

"More power to Operator 5!" she managed to say.

Rudolph fairly screamed with fury. The cords of his neck swelled so that they seemed about to burst. He seized the whip once more, and began to lash wildly, indiscriminately, at the heads, bodies, legs, of the two girls. The hard leather, which had previously been dipped in brine, bit deeply, scraping across raw flesh. But Rudolph did not stop. Long after the two girls had lost consciousness, long after they had died upon their crosses of torture, he continued to ply his whip, like a blind madman, until at last he fell, exhausted at the feet of the bodies of his two victims. He lay there, semi-conscious, all through the night, and none dared to enter the room until morning....

CHAPTER 8
AN ARMY IS BORN

THE EXPLOIT of Operator 5 in moving the ten ordnance trains a matter of almost a thousand miles, across the states of Missouri, Kansas and Colorado, through country swarming with Central Empire troops, is a matter of record, and cannot be disputed.

It has been said by students of military strategy that such a feat was possible only in a country like the United States, where the terrain and the vast stretches of land furnished ideal hiding places even for so large a convoy as ten trains—plus the spirit of a nation that never could be entirely broken. It was that spirit which brought recruits to the ordnance trains in their steady advance across the country—recruits in such numbers that soon Operator 5's forces had grown from a few paltry hundreds to more than twenty thousand.

For the first two days of the daring trek, the trains progressed slowly, pulling over, during the daylight hours, to little-used sidings under the shelter of towering mountain peaks. Here, the willing Americans collected brushwood and foliage, which they laboriously spread over the locomotives, the cars and the guns, so as to conceal them from the searching eyes of the countless Central Empire planes that combed the country for them. At night they moved on, after having received word from friendly Americans all along the line of travel as to the obstacles they might expect to encounter.

Always, they had a choice of one or more railroad lines which they might use, for the Central Empire found it impossible to keep all lines in constant use, and had abandoned all but the single system consisting of the Missouri Pacific, the Rock Island and the Union Pacific. This line was constantly in use and constantly patrolled, for supplies of all sorts were daily moving westward for the Imperial Armies in the Rockies. The Central Empire routed all its trains through St. Louis and Kansas City, thence by the Rock Island into Denver, and up to Cheyenne to hook into the Union Pacific track, thus going around the Continental Divide instead of through or over it.

They had abandoned altogether the Denver & Rio Grande Western, and the Denver & Salt Lake Lines, as being too exposed to sabotage by the Americans. The reason for this exposure to sabotage was, of course, that the former line used the Royal Gorge, where a shrewdly placed blast of dynamite could send a whole supply train toppling to destruction, while the latter line went through the Moffat Tunnel, under the Continental Divide, where another well-placed charge of high explosive could bring the whole mountainside down across the two ends of the tunnel, forming a living tomb for any convoy of troops that might be caught therein.

It was the first of two lines that Jimmy Christopher decided to use in the last great lap of the journey, the dash from Denver across the Colorado and Utah into Nevada.

Jimmy was planning every step carefully now, for the whole operation was assuming far greater proportions than its original intention. From a bold stroke of guerrilla warfare, the thing had grown to a great national undertaking which might eventually mean the checkmating of the Central Empire.

The news of the capture of those ordnance trains had spread all over the Occupied Territory, by that mysterious grapevine telegraph which the Purple conquerors could not understand or trace, but which worked as effectively as any system of organized communication.

And that news had fired the country. Volunteers began to meet the train in ever-increasing numbers at every stopping point. The twenty thousand recruits swelled to thirty, to forty thousand, to fifty thousand, and still increased.

After the second day, all possibility of or need for concealment had vanished, for Operator 5 found himself in command of an actual army.

HANK SHERIDAN was jubilant. For the first time since the Purple troops had moved down into New England in the early days of the invasion, there began to be some hope for America. In compartment A of Ordnance Train Number One, once the office of Colonel Henschel, now the field headquarters of the Continental Volunteer Army, as Sheridan called it, they held a council of war, poring over a military map.

"You see," Hank pointed out, "here's Arriba, where we are now. A few miles west, the main line of the Rock Island forks north and west. The northern branch goes right into Denver, while the southern one runs down to Colorado Springs and connects with the Denver & Rio Grande Western. I vote we divide our forces—half will go north and attack Denver, while the other half goes south!"

Jimmy Christopher shook his head. "No good, Hank. We'd only weaken ourselves by dividing up at this time. Napoleon won many of his battles by getting the enemy to divide their forces, then throwing his whole available forces against one of the halves. Our force is a comparatively small one, and we've got to keep it intact. You must remember that we're in enemy territory now, and that Marshal Kremer has at least a half million men in reserve behind the Front, which he can move against us. American civilians in Denver report that there are sixty or seventy thousand troops in and around Denver. We'd be outnumbered at the start. Our best bet is to take the southern fork, and cross the Royal Gorge. Then we can push on and perhaps contact Z-7 and the American Defense Force."

He turned to the others in the small compartment. "What is your opinion, gentlemen?"

The two other men present at this conference were Major General Homer Glanville, and Franklin Ransom, the inventor. Major General Glanville was a regular army officer who was at present serving with Z-7 at the Front, and who had flown to meet Operator 5 here.* Franklin Ransom was the noted inventor and metallurgist, winner of the Nobel Prize in chemistry, who was famed for his invention of *ransomite,* the super-lightweight metal alloy which made it possible to manufacture 155 mm guns that were so light they could be fired from an ordinary truck chassis with a special contrivance to take up the recoil.**

Major General Glanville was not a brilliant strategist, but he was an expert ordnance officer, and Jimmy Christopher had requested his presence here for the purpose of taking charge of the operation of the captured guns.

In answer to Jimmy's question, Glanville shrugged. "It's six of one and half a dozen of the other, Operator 5. If we lay siege to Denver, we've got the guns with which to do a good job. Those

---

* AUTHOR'S NOTE: At this time there was virtually no such organization as a regular army in the United States. At the inception of the Purple Invasion, the personnel of the Regular Army had been distributed among the newly formed divisions of American volunteers, to serve as officers in training the recruits. Several divisions of the regular army had been retained intact to act as shock troops in repelling the first wave of the invasion, and these divisions had been almost entirely wiped out in the first month of fighting. From then on, all warfare was conducted by volunteer divisions, and when Z-7, upon the death of the President of the United States, was put in supreme command of the American Defense Forces, he was wise enough to retain the advice and counsel of such of the experienced, professional soldiers as survived. Major General Glanville was one of these.

** AUTHOR'S NOTE: The story of Franklin Ransom was related in the novel entitled: "Siege of the Thousand Patriots."

Skodas that you captured are beauties. I've inspected every one of them, and they're in shipshape condition. There's enough ammunition on board these trains to lay down a twenty-four hour barrage. I have no doubt that we could drive the Purple troops out of Denver. But what could we do then? You have only about fifty thousand men, Operator 5. You couldn't hold Denver for any length of time, against the manpower that Kremer could throw against us."

He turned to Hank Sheridan. "I think Operator 5 is right. We should pass up Denver, and push through the Rocky Mountains. We need these guns over there. When I left Z-7 this morning, our Defense Force was in a bad position. As you know, we've been thrown back against the Sierra Nevadas. The enemy are in position at Salt Lake City, and all the territory west, to within a few miles of Carson City. We have no ammunition, and even if we did, our guns are no match for the enemy's. It's only a question of days before we must either surrender, or retreat to the ocean, leaving all the coast cities at the mercy of Kremer's armies. For that reason, I advise that we rush these guns westward as fast as possible!"

"All right," Hank Sheridan said, "I guess you're right. But how are we going to move an army of fifty thousand men through the enemy country? It was all right when we just had the Ordnance Trains to worry about—we didn't have to feed them. But fifty thousand men eat a helluva lot!"

"I think we can stop worrying about that, Hank," Jimmy said thoughtfully. "The civilians and the farmers wherever we pass are bringing more and more food supplies to us as we go along.

The whole country seems to be waking up. Truckloads of vegetables and freshly killed meat are being driven in every day. The enemy can't find a thing when they go foraging, so they have to maintain a communication line back to the east. That's where we have the advantage of them—we can get food as we go."

Hank Sheridan chuckled. "Not only that, but new volunteers are coming in by the hour—and bringing their own trucks and cars. It's amazing how many motor vehicles were hidden out from the enemy, when they were going around and commandeering transportation. Why, we could almost call ourselves a motorized army. There's enough transportation to carry all our men across the country—provided we can pick up gas and oil."

"There's an enemy gasoline supply base at Salida, right on the edge of the National Forest," General Glanville put in. "I think we'd have little trouble in taking that. They've got enough gasoline there to carry us clear across to the coast."

"That settles it," Jimmy Christopher said with sudden decision. "We start for the Rockies at once. We'll swing south through Colorado Springs and Pueblo, then west across the Royal Gorge. The trains will follow the Denver & Rio Grande, and the trucks and troops will use the roads, keeping pace with the trains. Hank, send out a strong advance force, to attack Colorado Springs and Pueblo. Give them a dozen of the Skoda guns, on a special train. They can have four hours' start. By the time our main body arrives there, I'll expect those two towns to be in our hands."

Hank Sheridan grinned sourly. "I'll take charge of that advance force myself. It'll be a pleasure to sock it into those

Central Empire babies for a change, instead of being on the receiving end the way we've been for the last eight months.

"General Glanville," Jimmy requested, "will you be good enough to detach the necessary guns and ammunition to accompany Hank's column, and to see that he is provided with competent gunners and artillery officers."

"Right, sir," said Glanville, and he saluted and left. Jimmy Christopher's affectionate glance followed the general's stalwart back as he walked from the compartment.

OPERATOR 5 looked out of the car window at the encampment of American volunteers which spread out almost as far as the eye could reach on both sides of the railroad tracks. Already there was a visible difference in the aspect of these Americans. No longer did they view matters with the hopeless, fatalistic attitude of a few days ago. Of course, they had been brave enough all through the invasion, but their words and thoughts and actions had been actuated by the spirit of self-sacrifice in an almost hopeless cause.

Now, however, they saw the nucleus of a new army, provided with guns and ammunition—an army strong enough to march boldly through enemy territory, and to fight on its own in the open, instead of pursuing the guerrilla warfare of the past few months. These men would still gladly die if necessary, in the service of their country; but would die now with a smile upon their lips, and hope in their breasts, for they began to see a glimmer of light in the darkness.

Though it was true that the American Defense Force in the Rockies was on the verge of surrender, they realized that the spirit of America—a spirit which had suddenly caused a whole army to blossom forth where there had only been a subjugated people before—was a spirit that must in the end be victorious, no matter how it was trampled upon in the meantime. And all through the annals of history, that pride of country had meant the difference between the survival and the extinction of nations.

So, at this moment, though the news from Z-7 was black, Jimmy Christopher held high hope for the emancipation of the United States.

While Hank Sheridan was preparing to leave with his contingent, and while Glanville supervised the cutting out of the cars carrying those guns which would be of best service in the undertaking, Operator 5 went into the next compartment, where Tim Donovan sat at the selfsame radio that Diane Elliot had been operating only a few days before when she had been surprised by Colonel Henschel.

Diane, together with Mamie Sandvik and a few of the other women, was busy in the encampment, planning and preparing the meals for the volunteer army. Tim Donovan had taken over the task of keeping in touch with Z-7 and with the American scouts by radio.

Now, the lad raised troubled eyes to Operator 5. "Gosh, Jimmy, I was just talking to P39 in New York.* He's been off

---

* AUTHOR'S NOTE: P39 was the Intelligence Department's code designation for Jack Peters, one of the most capable agents in the country. Before the Purple Invasion he had been engaged in counter-espionage work within the United States, and shortly after the Central Empire troops had occu-

the air for a week, because the Central Empire Surveillance Department discovered his antenna and raided his home. He escaped, and built another amateur set in one of the abandoned stations of the Sixth Avenue Elevated in Manhattan, and I just caught his signal.

"He tells me that Rudolph left for Denver two days ago, by plane. The Emperor was taken with an apoplectic fit when he discovered that we had seized these ordnance trains, and he's been ordering executions right and left. He's increased the reward on your head, and on Diane. They're arresting Americans by the hundreds in every city, and lining them up in front of firing squads!"

pied New England and New York, P39 had set himself up as a shoemaker in New York City, remaining under the rule of the conqueror. Throughout the eight months of the invasion he had stuck at his post, communicating by every imaginable means with the American headquarters, except for two periods when he had gone on special missions. There were thousands of Americans in every section of the country who had set up amateur radios in little-suspected spots, and who sent news over the land. It was through these amateur radio fans that Jimmy Christopher and Z-7 were enabled to keep abreast of happenings in every part of the Occupied Territory, and to have accurate knowledge of the movements of enemy troops. Thus, while the Central Empire High Command was more than once taken by surprise, the American Defense Forces never were without information as to what might be expected to happen. This was a great factor in prolonging the resistance. It must be remembered that no other country in the world had been able to withstand the Purple Armies for as long as eight months.

Jimmy Christopher's hands clenched at his sides. "God!" he bit out. "When will that Imperial Beast stop slaughtering our people? I have half a mind to change our plans and attack Denver instead of going on west!"

"Take it easy, Jimmy," Tim Donovan warned. "I heard what was said in your compartment, through Diane's dictograph. You and General Glanville agreed there's nothing to be gained by attacking Denver. You'd stand little chance of catching Rudolph, and you'd put this whole army that you've built up in danger of being wiped out. But something has to be done about that Emperor. P39 told me that he whipped two young girls to death with a cowhide whip the day he heard about the ordnance trains. He beat them until they died! Can you imagine it, Jimmy? They were only kids—fifteen or sixteen years old!"

Jimmy Christopher's eyes blazed. His lips clamped together, and he gulped hard. "Fifteen years old! My God, they were only children!"

Suddenly, with a look of hard decision in his face, he squared his shoulders and raised his right hand. "Tim, I swear here and now, by all that I hold sacred, that if the Central Empire isn't driven out of America within thirty days, I will myself go to Rudolph's headquarters, and either kill him, or die in the attempt. By God, that man deserves less mercy than a mad dog!"

Tim Donovan's eyes were glittering. "I take half of that oath, Jimmy! When you go, I'll go with you!"

Solemnly, the two clasped hands, sealing their bargain with fate….

Shortly afterward, Hank Sheridan, with a detachment of

ten thousand American volunteers, left the main column for their sally against Colorado Springs and Pueblo. A ten-car ordnance train was shunted ahead over a side track, and sent forward, to accompany them. The train consisted of three flat-cars each carrying a great Skoda gun, two flatcars upon which were mounted long, graceful anti-aircraft guns, and five cars of supplies and ammunition. At the last moment, General Glan-ville decided to accompany the expedition as chief artillery officer. They left amid the cheers of the remaining men. Jimmy Christopher shook hands with Glanville and Sheridan.

Glanville said: "According to the reports from our scouts, there should be little opposition either in Colorado Springs or in Pueblo. We shouldn't have any difficulty in taking both towns."

Jimmy nodded, turned to Sheridan. "As you move along, Hank, leave men posted on the railroad as well as on the auto-mobile road; string them out at sufficient intervals so that they will be within sight of each other, and can relay signals in case a body of enemy troops should appear anywhere along the line after you pass. In that way, the main column here will know exactly what it can expect to encounter when it starts to move."

"Right, Jimmy," Hank said. "And I'll radio back to you every fifteen minutes. Keep Tim at the earphones."

Jimmy Christopher watched the long column of trucks and autos wind along the automobile road, with the ordnance train pacing them on the railroad tracks three hundred feet away. According to reports of scouts he knew that the column would always be within sight of the train until they reached Colorado Springs, so that they could cooperate closely.

According to arrangements, the main body was to start out within four hours. If Hank's expedition should encounter any unforeseen difficulties, or should find itself opposed by a superior body of the enemy, the main column could come to its support in ample time.

CHAPTER 9
FIRST VICTORY!

T HE STORY of Hank Sheridan's Expedition is well known to every student of history. It was marked by two pitched battles in as many hours.

The first took place some twenty-five or thirty miles from Colorado Springs, on the banks of Black Squirrel Creek. The first intimation of trouble came when Hank Sheridan, riding in the lead car of the column, glanced up to the north, and noticed a black speck in the sky.

He frowned, and watched the speck grow steadily larger until he could recognize it as one of the new two-motored Fallada Scout Planes, which the Central Empire had recently put into use. These Falladas were powerful, vicious fighting machines, equipped with two machine guns on the wings and two more that synchronized with the propellers. The guns on the wings could be swiveled about to fire in any direction, by means of a small lever in the observer's seat, while the pilot manipulated the two forward guns. In addition, there was a built-in bomb compartment, carrying four shells, which could be dropped one at a time by means of individual trapdoors under the fuselage.

116

They were the very last thing in aerial fighting equipment, and had been developed by the Central Empire to counteract the flotilla of planes which Jimmy Christopher had managed to buy in South America some months ago.

Hank Sheridan watched anxiously while the Fallada came roaring toward them. He snapped to his aide, who sat beside him in the rear of the car: "Hines! Signal the train to prepare the anti-aircraft guns for action! Halt the column!"

Hines jumped to relay Hank's order, and the long column ground to a halt behind them, while a signalman flagged the train by semaphore. Immediately the airbrakes screamed as the train slowed down, and they could see the slim anti-aircraft guns swiveling about on the flatcars.

But the Fallada did not approach near enough to drop any bombs. It circled once, at a distance, as if to give the observer a better view of the column, then it banked and flew swiftly northward again.

Hanks brow furrowed. "He's seen all he needs to see," he growled. "I bet we'll have a swarm of those hornets around our heads in a few minutes! He's probably gone to get his squadron!"

The column had just crossed the narrow wooden bridge across the river, and Hank ordered his signalman to signal the man they had left behind to relay the news of the scout plane to Jimmy Christopher. But Hines gripped his arm. "Look, sir! Across the bridge! There's infantry coming!"

It was true enough. Long ranks of Central Empire infantry, accompanied by a squadron of armored motorcycles, had appeared in the road around the bend on the other side of the

The motorcycle was catapulted into the air, a twisted mass of metal.

bridge. They were advancing at the double quick, and even as he watched the enemy approach, Hank heard the insistent droning of a flight of planes. Looking up to the north, he saw squadron after squadron of Falladas roaring toward them, in echelon formation.

The enemy must have been close by when Hank's column

passed on the other side of the river. The Purple troops were already firing as they advanced, and several of the Americans dropped under the hail of lead.

Hank issued swift orders, and the Americans spread out on both sides of the road, concentrating their fire on the bridgehead to prevent the enemy from crossing.

The Americans were taken at a disadvantage, because the

Central Empire planes would be able to bomb them, driving them back from the bridge until the infantry had crossed. Already the Falladas were almost overhead, but they were driven to higher altitude by the anti-aircraft guns on the train, which attempted to bracket them.

HINES PLUCKED at Hank Sheridan's sleeve. "They'll drive us back from the bridge, sir, if they can dive under the archie fire. And if the enemy infantry crosses the bridge, we'll have to defend ourselves on the ground while they bomb us from the air—"

Hank nodded, comprehending the situation. Already, one of the armored motorcycles of the enemy had swung on to the bridge, and was moving slowly across, impervious to the rifle and machine-gun fire of the Americans.

"Only one thing to do," Hank decided quickly. "We got to destroy that bridge!" He leaped into his car, shouted to the driver: "Turn around and drive back to the bridge! Fast, man!"

The driver obeyed, and in a moment the car was speeding back along the road, past the halted column, toward the bridge. Hank leaned down and extracted a grenade from a box on the floorboard. As the car screeched to a stop within twenty feet of the bridge. Hank leaped out, raced ahead, at the same time pulling the pin from the grenade. The enemy motorcycle was already half way across with flame and lead spitting from the machine gun behind its armored shield. Bullets whined around Hank Sheridan's ears as he hurled the grenade directly at the motorcycle.

It exploded even as it struck, and the motorcycle was literally catapulted into the air, a twisted mass of metal, while a great gaping hole appeared across the bridge.

The wooden planks sank out of sight for a moment, only to reappear again, floating downstream. A second motorcycle, speeding after the first, dived into the water before its driver could stop it. The enemy infantry stopped on the farther bank, staring at the gap in the bridge. The way was barred by Hank Sheridan's swift action.

The planes had flown directly over the column, but they had been forced so high by the archie guns that the bombs they dropped fell far wide of the road. Now they turned, in perfect formation, and came back, dropping a little lower for the second load.

If the pilots of those planes were emboldened to reduce their altitude by the thought that the Americans manning the anti-aircraft guns were not regular artillerists, but only civilian volunteers, they were due for a sad disillusionment. Major General Glanville was an old hand with anti-aircraft guns, and the men he had chosen for this detail were all veteran gunners.

No sooner had the planes dipped than the long guns began to belch once more, and this time the enemy planes were perfectly bracketed! The first squadron flew directly into the hail of archie fire before they understood that the Americans had the range to perfection.

The planes behind crashed into the first squadron, and the locked flaming ships fell in a dreadful cataclysm of destruction.

The second and third squadrons of Falladas pulled out of their course frantically to avoid being involved in the crash, and they banked around to head out of the area of danger. But so skillfully had General Glanville set the range that the planes were virtually hemmed in by a circle of archie fire, gradually narrowing inexorably.

The panic-stricken pilots attempted to obtain altitude, but three of every four of them were brought down. The survivors put their tails between their legs and fled.

The infantry on the other side of the bridge were already in retreat, realizing that they could be wiped out by gunfire from the train, now that they no longer had aerial support. But General Glanville swung two of the great Skoda guns into action, and shells burst among the fleeing Purple Troopers, taking fearful toll. They were retreating, not in the direction from which they had come, but back up the road toward Limon. They were sure to meet the main body of the Americans under Jimmy Christopher, and would be wiped out completely.

General Glanville let them go, only taking the precaution of radioing back to Operator 5 to warn him.

Wild shouts went up from the Americans as they realized that they had won an engagement with the enemy within the space of ten minutes—and had won it with the loss of only a few lives!

This was what the Americans had needed. For eight months now they had fought with their backs to the wall, never daring to meet the enemy in a pitched battle, because the enemy's equipment was always superior. Now they had had a chance to see what the Central Empire soldiers were made of, how they stood up when the odds were more nearly equal than they had been at any time during the past eight months. And they were filled with a great contempt for those goose-stepping, gray-clad troops who had built up a huge legendary reputation for invincibility when they marched victoriously over Europe and Asia, and then came to America to repeat the performance.

Those troopers were not the invincible fighters that the world believed them to be. Give them better guns, better equipment, better generalship than other soldiers, and they would march to conquest; but pit them on equal terms against Americans, and they fled ignominiously. The news of that engagement, filtering out by the grapevine telegraph to the hinterlands of the Occupied Territory, did more to bolster up the courage and the hope of Americans, in the dark days that were to follow, than any other single thing.

Thus, the Battle of El Paso County, as it came to be known, holds a high place in our history, not because it was important in itself, but because it enabled the Americans to bear with greater fortitude the trying days that were to follow.

IT DID not take Hank Sheridan's column long to re-form, and resume its march. But now there was a difference. Many of these Americans had never participated in an engagement before. Now they had been through their first fire, and they had won a victory. They felt that they were veterans. And they began to feel a surge of confidence in their leaders. If any of them had been skeptical about marching under other leadership than that of Operator 5, they had lost that skepticism in their admiration for the quick thinking and courageous action of Hank Sheridan in blowing up the bridge, and for the superb gunnery of General Glanville.

And so, as they marched, there was a spring in their step, and a song at their lips. They were looking forward to their next tussle. It came at Colorado Springs, and served only to increase their spirits.

Here, almost under the shadow of Pike's Peak, General Glanville set up his long guns, which, being of newer manufacture, outranged those of the Central Empire in Colorado Springs and on Pike's Peak by almost twenty per cent. Fifteen minutes of bombardment brought an officer with a white flag. They would surrender the City as well as Pike's Peak, provided they were permitted to march away with their arms and with colors flying.

Hank Sheridan and General Glanville were filled with a fierce joy. Both of them knew very well that any garrison of Americans, even though they might have been raw recruits, would never have surrendered after fifteen minutes of the most intense shelling. They both recalled the story of the siege of Mount Washington, where Americans had withstood constant drumfire for a week until they drove the enemy away by a clever ruse.*

It only went to prove that the Purple troops were really inferior soldiers, able to fight only when the odds were on their side.

---

* AUTHOR'S NOTE: The story of the attack by the enemy on the American position at Mount Washington, together with the details of the manner in which they were able to raise the siege and rout a numerically superior enemy, was related under the title of "The Siege of the Thousand Patriots."

At a single bold stroke, the Americans had seized a most important strategic point, and were the masters of the road to the west!

From Colorado Springs, Hank found that there was a perfectly good single-track standard gauge railway leading directly to the Royal Gorge, and that they would not have to detour through Pueblo. So he communicated the results of the battle to Jimmy Christopher, who was already on the march, having met and taken prisoner the remnants of the enemy troops fleeing from the Battle of El Paso County. Jimmy Christopher wired his congratulations and continued on, while Hank Sheridan, now a sort of glorified advance guard, marched proudly at the head of his new-made veterans to drive the enemy from the bridge over the Royal Gorge, thus opening the road to Salida, where the enemy kept its gasoline stores.

The triumphal progress of the American Revolutionary Army had begun!

More recruits flocked to Operator 5's banner, and the army crossed the Continental Divide almost a hundred thousand strong!

CHAPTER 10
THE ARMY
WITHOUT A COUNTRY

JIMMY CHRISTOPHER sat in Compartment B of the Pullman car of Ordnance Train Number One, talking with Diane Elliot and Tim Donovan, who had not left the radio since the morning. The reports had been coming in steadily from Hank Sheridan, and the volunteers on the trains, as well as those on the road in the trucks, were singing lustily. Before them all there began to arise the vision of a once more free United States, of homes that might resume normal routine some day soon, of the patient, hardworking days of reconstruction that would follow after the invader had been driven from our shores.

Jimmy Christopher looked out of the window of the compartment, and his eyes glowed warmly at the sight of the happy Americans in the truck on the road which paralleled the railroad tracks. Above the advancing column, his eyes spotted the single plane, piloted by Kelton, the aviator, who had flown Jimmy to Sedalia. That plane constituted the entire air force of the American Revolutionary Army at the present time. He smiled slowly, and was about to speak to Diane, when the radio at Tim's elbow suddenly came to life.

They both waited while Tim adjusted his earphones and picked up Z-7's signal. Jimmy Christopher smiled across at Diane, drinking in her pale, fragile beauty, and wondering what he would do if he were ever to be deprived of her. He was relaxing now, after twenty-four hours without sleep, but he did not feel in the least sleepy. The excitement of their spectacular success so far was still driving sleep from his eyes.

It was one of those bitter jests of fate that at the only moment in the last eight months when Operator 5 might have felt some measure of contentment, of satisfaction at success, the worst blow of all should fall. Certain it is that neither he nor Diane suspected that this instant, while Tim Donovan was catching

Z-7's call letters, would be the last moment of relaxation they would have for many a weary day.

THE FIRST inkling Jimmy had that there was anything wrong was when he heard Tim Donovan's sharp intake of breath as the lad listened to the sharp voice of Z-7 through the earphones.

That intake of breath was sibilant, like that of a man who has been struck a mortal blow.

Diane stiffened, and Jimmy Christopher tensed. "Tim! What's up?"

Tim Donovan turned stricken eyes to him. The boy's face had drained of all color, and his lower lip was trembling. He tried to speak, but only a moan of mental agony came from his pallid lips.

Violently he tore the earphones from his head, thrust them at Jimmy, and pushed out of his seat.

Operator 5 looked at him queerly, took the earphones and adjusted them, then sat down at the radio. He caught Z-7's voice, weighted down, like the shoulders of a man bearing a cross.

"Tim! Why don't you answer? Tim—"

"This is Operator 5, Z-7," Jimmy Christopher said slowly. "What's happened? Tim seems on the verge of collapse. And your voice sounds—"

He stopped as words, jumbled, hopeless, deadened, floated through the ether. "Jimmy! I—I had to tell you this myself. I—I couldn't trust anyone else to—tell you. I've arranged—for the American Defense Force to surrender to Marshal Kremer at dawn!"

PATRIOTS' DEATH MARCH

As the plant hurtled into the side of the blimp,
the slipstream whipped Jimmy's parachute open.

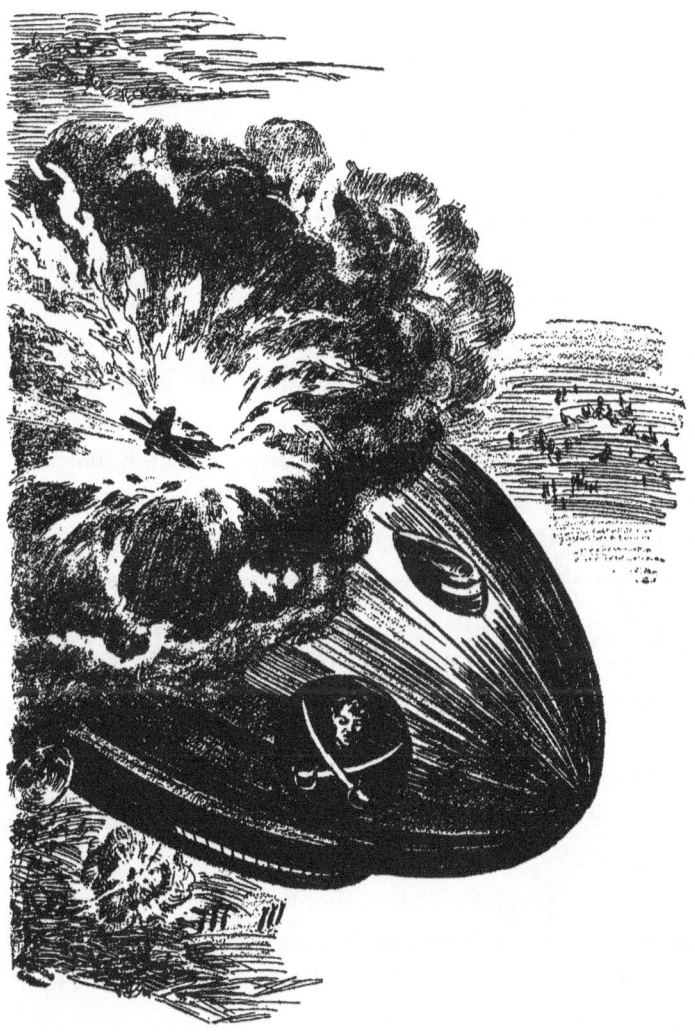

"What?" The word cracked from Jimmy Christopher's lips like a pistol shot.

"It's true, Jimmy. I—couldn't—hold out any longer. We had not a single round of ammunition left. The men were dying under the enemy bombardment like flies. Our food supplies from the north and the south have been cut off, and the civilians in the coast cities are starving as well as the men at the Front."

"But, man alive!" Jimmy shouted. "How could you do it? A couple of days more, that's all we'd have needed. We're fighting our way through and I've got a hundred thousand men. I've got guns. We could have driven the enemy back—"

"I'm sorry, Jimmy, but I couldn't hold out. They—brought pressure to bear on me. They showed me starving women and children. They said the lives of those poor innocents would be on my head. They said there was no use defending a narrow strip of coast line against the might of the Central Empire. I've gotten fairly good terms from Kremer. He's promised there won't be any wholesale executions. The men will be allowed to lay down their arms and go home. John Coburn, the President of the Board of Governors, is to be made regent of the country under Rudolph's jurisdiction. And, more important than anything else, the women and children will be fed."

Jimmy Christopher groaned. "Just when we began to see a light. Z-7, *how* could you do it?"

"I don't know, I don't know. They kept at me, day in, day out, hour after hour, telling me I was responsible for every man who died at the Front. And the hell of it is that they were right. It wasn't war any more, it was slaughter. The boys just stood there and waited for the shrapnel to come, and then when they couldn't hold a position any longer, they'd have to move back, and wait for the enemy artillery to catch up with them again. I lost ninety thousand men today. That's what broke up my resistance."

Z-7's voice cracked, and suddenly the air became silent.

Jimmy Christopher tore the earphones from his head, turned to find Tim and Diane staring at him. Diane had grasped the situation from the tenor of the conversation. She put a sympathetic hand on Operator 5's arm. "It couldn't be helped, Jimmy. If Z-7 surrendered, be sure it was the only thing to do."

Jimmy shook her arm off. "No, no. There must be some way out. We've got guns, an army here—"

"But no place to go," Tim broke in tartly. "Now that the American Defense Force has surrendered," he went on bitterly, "there's no place to go. We're an army without a country!"

"I'm not going to surrender," Jimmy Christopher said firmly. "By God, I'll keep on fighting!"

"What'll you do with the army?" Tim demanded. "Rudolph'll be able to turn three million men against your hundred thousand, now that there's no Front line. How long could you resist—"

"I can take the army into hiding," Jimmy insisted stubbornly. "With these men and guns as a nucleus, I could build up an organization—"

Tim Donovan was almost hysterical with the bitter disillusionment of the news of the surrender; and his very hysteria made him argue all the more. "Where would you hide? They'd find you—"

"Not in Death Valley!" Jimmy Christopher exclaimed. "They'd never find us in Death Valley. I could bring in enough food to last us for the winter—"

"How about water?" Tim cut in. "Could you bring in enough water—"

"Excuse me," a voice in the doorway broke in. "If I may be permitted to say a word?"

Jimmy whirled around, to find the inventor and metallurgist, Franklin Ransom, standing in the corridor.

Ransom smiled. "Forgive me if I intrude. I couldn't help overhearing the conversation." He fixed his piercing eyes on Jimmy Christopher. "Operator 5, if you really want to take up winter quarters in Death Valley, I think I can guarantee you a sufficient supply of water!"

Jimmy gasped: "How?"

"In my youth I was a prospector. I've been through Death Valley a hundred times. I've studied the geology of the district. And I'm convinced that with the proper equipment I could go down deep enough to tap water!"

Jimmy Christopher took a step forward. "This equipment—would it be difficult to get?"

Ransom smiled again. "Not if you're a good thief. You'd have to steal it from the Central Empire storehouses."

A slow smile spread over Jimmy's face. "Consider it done, Mr. Ransom. Our winter quarters are arranged for—practically."

A new vitality seemed to have entered Operator 5. He issued

swift orders. "Tim! Order the column to halt. Signal Kelton to bring the plane down, and when he does so, see that it's properly serviced and fueled for a thousand-mile hop. I'm flying to the coast to look the situation over personally. I want to talk to Z-7 if possible. I'll be back about noon tomorrow. In the meantime, join up with Hank Sheridan's column, and tell him what we intend to do. Work out the best route by which we can reach Death Valley, and send out scouts to chart the roads!"

"Yes *sir!*" Tim Donovan said with a sudden return of his good spirits. The sight of Jimmy Christopher in action was always a sure-fire method of raising the boy's spirits. He left, whistling Yankee Doodle.

THE GOLDEN plains of California reflected the warm glow of the dawn as Jimmy Christopher piloted Kelton's plane on a southwesterly course toward Sacramento. He had left Kelton behind, and had strapped the pilot's parachute on his back.

His face was grimly intent as he peered over the side of the ship, at the plain below. Thousands of Americans were marching in wide ranks, with slow, dispirited step. Jimmy could see that they were stacking their arms as he passed a reviewing stand where stood several American officers. Among those officers would be Z-7, and Operator 5's heart tightened, as he imagined the thoughts that must be running through the mind of the former Chief of Intelligence while he watched the last gesture of a beaten army.

Some ten miles back, Jimmy had passed the marching cohorts of the Central Empire, moving forward to accept the surrender of the American Defense Force. Soon they would be here, and Marshal Kremer, perhaps Rudolph himself, would accept Z-7's sword, in token of submission.

The few pitiful cannon and anti-aircraft guns of the Americans were parked in a wide field not far from the reviewing stand. They had been moved in from the front lines during the night, prepared for the ceremony. The Americans, Jimmy thought bitterly, were now utterly defenseless, utterly at the mercy of the Purple Emperor.

And almost as if in confirmation of that thought, a great black shadow fell athwart Jimmy's cockpit. Frowning, he raised his eyes, to see a huge blimp, one of the three in use by the Central Empire, sailing majestically far above him.

The blimp paid no attention to Jimmy's plane, for his wings were still painted with the insignia of the Central Empire, and the captain of the airship no doubt took him for one of their own pilots.

Jimmy banked to the south, seeking a place to land. If he was to talk to Z-7 he must do so quickly, otherwise his chance would be gone.

As Jimmy veered southward, the shadow of the blimp above him fell away. He rose a bit to get another look at that blimp, thinking that perhaps Rudolph might be on board. And just as he began to rise, he saw something that sent cold shivers up and down his spine.

From underneath the gondola of the blimp, a long, dark, cigar-shaped object suddenly dropped, speeding down toward the earth like a plummet.

Jimmy's eyes dilated. He knew what that was. It was a new type of aerial torpedo perfected by the Central Empire. It possessed destructive properties equal to those of five 155 mm shells, by reason of its soft casing. And it was hurtling down toward the sea of upturned faces on the plain below!

Jimmy's fascinated gaze followed that torpedo down to the earth, saw the men below running frantically to escape, saw it strike, and saw the geyser-like spray of earth that resulted from its explosion. The men down there looked very small from up here, and it seemed as if hundreds of little ants were being hurled about by the detonation. They were in reality human beings who had been blown up—men of the surrendered American Defense Force.

Jimmy Christopher uttered a choked cry. So this was the word of Marshal Kremer! This was what his promise meant! Now that the Americans were helpless, at their mercy, they were amusing themselves by dropping torpedoes among them!

Another black object left the bottom of the gondola, went spiraling downward, exploded among the helpless men. JIMMY'S JAWS clamped tightly together, and his eyes burned with indignation. Never had he seen so callous an action on the part of a conqueror among civilized nations. Savage tribes of warriors in India had been known to massacre the garrisons of towns which had surrendered, but such an act had never been committed by a civilized nation.

While these thoughts raced through his brain, he had swung into swift action. Pulling his stick far back, viciously, he rose sharply, the wind screaming in his wings, and the slipstream beating at his face. Up, up he rose, until he had attained altitude. The crew of the blimp saw him pass them, and waved to him from the gondola, thinking that he was stunting in celebration of their abominable action. And even as he passed them, he saw another one of those destructive torpedoes loosed on his way downward.

He leveled off above the blimp, looked down and saw men on the ground running frantically in every direction to escape the third torpedo. But the field was so crowded that there was no escape for the unfortunate Americans. It burst among them, sending bombs, blood and bone flying in every direction.

Operator 5 knew that the blimp carried at least twenty of these compact torpedoes, and it was evidently their intention to drop their entire load. He resolved grimly that he would never permit it.

He banked once more, pushed his stick forward, and descended in a lightning-swift power-dive, headed directly for the blimp. He pulled the trips of his machine guns to test them, and waited for the burst.

None came!

He frowned, pulled the trips again. The guns did not respond. He remembered with startling vividness that Kelton had told him he was out of machine-gun ammunition, and could not get any because the guns were special type Brownings, the ammunition for which was no longer available since the American factories had been seized by the Central Empire.

By this time he was almost upon the blimp, and he could see the horrified expressions of the crew in the gondola. At least he had accomplished this much so far—he had frightened them out of dropping the next torpedo for the moment.

With a quick dexterous motion he pulled back the stick, dragging the ship out of its headlong power dive. The struts whined, and he felt the strain against the wings. For a moment he thought he would not be able to level off, but he breathed a sigh of relief as the plane righted itself.

He climbed again, got altitude once more. He couldn't use his machine guns against that blimp, but he was determined that no more men should be slaughtered down below.

He descended until he was at the same altitude as the blimp, then banked, and headed directly for it. He locked the stick in its position, saw that the plane would hold its course. Then without hesitation, he put a leg over the side, and leaped out!

He felt the pull of the forward motion of the plane against his body, then he lost the forward momentum, and began to plummet downward. He pulled the rip-cord of the parachute, and just at that moment his ears were fairly deafened by the reverberations of a thunderous explosion from above. The plane had crashed into the blimp!

Jimmy felt his downward plunge suddenly broken as the parachute billowed out above him. He hung idly in the air, descending slowly, while a great mass of flaming wreckage whirled down past him. It was the burning blimp.

He had done it!

Twenty minutes later, a car picked him up from the field where he had come down, whirled him swiftly to the reviewing stand at the edge of the field that the blimp had been strafing.

The enemy had not yet arrived, and the great throng of American soldiers broke into vociferous cheers at his arrival. Z-7, his eyes wet, led him up to the stand, where a dozen army officers shook his hand.

It was almost ten minutes before he could break away from their congratulations to draw Z-7 aside. The Intelligence Chief avoided his gaze.

"Jimmy, I know what you must think of me. But it's too late now. Even if I wanted to recall the surrender, I couldn't do it. We're helpless now."

"I know, Z-7, I know. I don't blame you. I know what pressure must have been brought to bear upon you."

"Then—you're—you're going to surrender too?"

"Not by a long shot, Z-7!" Swiftly, Jimmy told him of his plans to winter in Death Valley, to build up the strength of the American Revolutionary Army.

The two men shook hands, gazing for a long time into each other's eyes.

Jimmy Christopher whispered: "To a New America, Z-7!" *

* AUTHOR'S NOTE: The dash to Death Valley, following close upon the eleventh-hour escape of the main American army from capitulation to the armies of the Purple Emperor, constituted one of the most amazing maneuvers of military history. That great expanse of arid waste, the burial ground of American pioneers and prospectors for a century, became an armed camp, ringed by the steel of Marshal Kremer's veterans and stalked by the twin specters of starvation and thirst. Operator 5's stupendous task was to hold this ground and plug the gaps in a riddled battle front. Intrigue and adventure intermingle in this historic narrative, told in the next installment.

THE SPIDER

- ❏ #1: The Spider Strikes — $13.95
- ❏ #2: The Wheel of Death — $13.95
- ❏ #3: Wings of the Black Death — $13.95
- ❏ #4: City of Flaming Shadows — $13.95
- ❏ #5: Empire of Doom! — $13.95
- ❏ #6: Citadel of Hell — $13.95
- ❏ #7: The Serpent of Destruction — $13.95
- ❏ #8: The Mad Horde — $13.95
- ❏ #9: Satan's Death Blast — $13.95
- ❏ #10: The Corpse Cargo — $13.95
- ❏ #11: Prince of the Red Looters — $13.95
- ❏ #12: Reign of the Silver Terror — $13.95
- ❏ #13: Builders of the Dark Empire — $13.95
- ❏ #14: Death's Crimson Juggernaut — $13.95
- ❏ #15: The Red Death Rain — $13.95
- ❏ #16: The City Destroyer — $13.95
- ❏ #17: The Pain Emperor — $13.95
- ❏ #18: The Flame Master — $13.95
- ❏ #19: Slaves of the Crime Master — $13.95
- ❏ #20: Reign of the Death Fiddler — $13.95
- ❏ #21: Hordes of the Red Butcher — $13.95
- ❏ #22: Dragon Lord of the Underworld — $13.95
- ❏ #23: Master of the Death-Madness — $13.95
- ❏ #24: King of the Red Killers — $13.95
- ❏ #25: Overlord of the Damned — $13.95
- ❏ #26: Death Reign of the Vampire King — $13.95
- ❏ #27: Emperor of the Yellow Death — $13.95
- ❏ #28: The Mayor of Hell — $13.95
- ❏ #29: Slaves of the Murder Syndicate — $13.95
- ❏ #30: Green Globes of Death — $13.95
- ❏ #31: The Cholera King — $13.95
- ❏ #32: Slaves of the Dragon — $13.95
- ❏ #33: Legions of Madness — $12.95
- ❏ #34: Laboratory of the Damned — $12.95
- ❏ #35: Satan's Sightless Legion — $12.95
- ❏ #36: The Coming of the Terror — $12.95
- ❏ #37: The Devil's Death-Dwarfs — $12.95
- ❏ #38: City of Dreadful Night — $12.95
- ❏ #39: Reign of the Snake Men — $12.95
- ❏ #40: Dictator of the Damned — $12.95
- ❏ #41: The Mill-Town Massacres — $12.95
- ❏ #42: Satan's Workshop — $12.95
- ❏ #43: Scourge of the Yellow Fangs — $12.95
- ❏ #44: The Devil's Pawnbroker — $12.95
- ❏ #45: Voyage of the Coffin Ship — $12.95
- ❏ #46: The Man Who Ruled in Hell — $13.95
- ❏ #47: Slaves of the Black Monarch — $13.95
- ❏ #48: Machineguns Over the White House — $13.95
- ❏ #49: The City That Dared Not Eat — $13.95
- ❏ #50: Master of the Flaming Horde — $13.95
- ❏ #51: Satan's Switchboard — $13.95
- ❏ #52: Legions of the Accursed Light — $13.95
- ❏ #53: The City of Lost Men — $13.95
- ❏ #54: The Grey Horde Creeps — $13.95
- ❏ #55: City of Whispering Death — $13.95
- ❏ #56: When Thousands Slept in Hell — $13.95
- ❏ **NEW:** #57: Satan's Shakles — $14.95

THE WESTERN RAIDER

- ❏ #1: Guns of the Damned — $13.95
- ❏ #2: The Hawk Rides Back from Death — $13.95
- ❏ #3: Gun-Call for the Lost Legion — $13.95
- ❏ #4: The Law of Silver Trent — $13.95
- ❏ #5: The Gun-Prayer of Silver Trent — $13.95
- ❏ #6: Silver Trent Rides Alone — $13.95

G-8 AND HIS BATTLE ACES

- ❏ #1: The Bat Staffel — $13.95

CAPTAIN SATAN

- ❏ #1: The Mask of the Damned — $13.95
- ❏ #2: Parole for the Dead — $13.95
- ❏ #3: The Dead Man Express — $13.95
- ❏ #4: A Ghost Rides the Dawn — $13.95
- ❏ #5: The Ambassador From Hell — $13.95

DR. YEN SIN

- ❏ #1: Mystery of the Dragon's Shadow — $12.95
- ❏ #2: Mystery of the Golden Skull — $12.95
- ❏ #3: Mystery of the Singing Mummies — $12.95

POPULAR HERO PULPS AVAILABLE NOW:

CAPTAIN COMBAT
- ❏ #1: The Sky Beast of Berlin — $13.95
- ❏ #2: Red Wings For the Blood Battalion — $13.95
- ❏ #3: Low Ceiling For Nazi Hell Hawks — $13.95

OPERATOR 5
- ❏ #1: The Masked Invasion — $13.95
- ❏ #2: The Invisible Empire — $13.95
- ❏ #3: The Yellow Scourge — $13.95
- ❏ #4: The Melting Death — $13.95
- ❏ #5: Cavern of the Damned — $13.95
- ❏ #6: Master of Broken Men — $13.95
- ❏ #7: Invasion of the Dark Legions — $13.95
- ❏ #8: The Green Death Mists — $13.95
- ❏ #9: Legions of Starvation — $13.95
- ❏ #10: The Red Invader — $13.95
- ❏ #11: The League of War-Monsters — $13.95
- ❏ #12: The Army of the Dead — $13.95
- ❏ #13: March of the Flame Marauders — $13.95
- ❏ #14: Blood Reign of the Dictator — $13.95
- ❏ #15: Invasion of the Yellow Warlords — $13.95
- ❏ #16: Legions of the Death Master — $13.95
- ❏ #17: Hosts of the Flaming Death — $13.95
- ❏ #18: Invasion of the Crimson Death Cult — $13.95
- ❏ #19: Attack of the Blizzard Men — $13.95
- ❏ #20: Scourge of the Invisible Death — $13.95
- ❏ #21: Raiders of the Red Death — $13.95
- ❏ #22: War-Dogs of the Green Destroyer — $13.95
- ❏ #23: Rockets From Hell — $13.95
- ❏ #24: War-Masters from the Orient — $13.95
- ❏ #25: Crime's Reign of Terror — $13.95
- ❏ #26: Death's Ragged Army — $13.95
- ❏ #27: Patriots' Death Battalion — $13.95
- ❏ #28: The Bloody Forty-five Days — $13.95
- ❏ #29: America's Plague Battalions — $13.95
- ❏ #30: Liberty's Suicide Legions — $13.95
- ❏ #31: Siege of the Thousand Patriots — $13.95
- ❏ **NEW:** #32: Patriots' Death March — $14.95

DUSTY AYRES AND HIS BATTLE BIRDS
- ❏ #1: Black Lightning! — $13.95
- ❏ #2: Crimson Doom — $13.95
- ❏ #3: The Purple Tornado — $13.95
- ❏ #4: The Screaming Eye — $13.95
- ❏ #5: The Green Thunderbolt — $13.95
- ❏ #6: The Red Destroyer — $13.95
- ❏ #7: The White Death — $13.95
- ❏ #8: The Black Avenger — $13.95
- ❏ #9: The Silver Typhoon — $13.95
- ❏ #10: The Troposphere F-S — $13.95
- ❏ #11: The Blue Cyclone — $13.95
- ❏ #12: The Tesla Raiders — $13.95

MAVERICKS
- ❏ #1: Five Against the Law — $12.95
- ❏ #2: Mesquite Manhunters — $12.95
- ❏ #3: Bait for the Lobo Pack — $12.95
- ❏ #4: Doc Grimson's Outlaw Posse — $12.95
- ❏ #5: Charlie Parr's Gunsmoke Cure — $12.95

THE MYSTERIOUS WU FANG
- ❏ #1: The Case of the Six Coffins — $12.95
- ❏ #2: The Case of the Scarlet Feather — $12.95
- ❏ #3: The Case of the Yellow Mask — $12.95
- ❏ #4: The Case of the Suicide Tomb — $12.95
- ❏ #5: The Case of the Green Death — $12.95
- ❏ #6: The Case of the Black Lotus — $12.95
- ❏ #7: The Case of the Hidden Scourge — $12.95

THE SECRET 6
- ❏ #1: The Red Shadow — $13.95
- ❏ #2: House of Walking Corpses — $13.95
- ❏ #3: The Monster Murders — $13.95
- ❏ #4: The Golden Alligator — $13.95

CAPTAIN ZERO
- ❏ #1: City of Deadly Sleep — $13.95
- ❏ #2: The Mark of Zero! — $13.95
- ❏ #3: The Golden Murder Syndicate — $13.95

www.ingramcontent.com/pod-product-compliance
Lightning Source LLC
Chambersburg PA
CBHW020624250626
47154CB00004B/1659